GOOD ENOUGH IN A PINCH

MARCOS ANTONIO HERNANDEZ

CHAPTER ONE

EVERY PAIR of blue eyes in the Gamma district market sneaks quick glances through the haze overhead, scanning for falling parts of the hovercrafts being shot down that could land on their heads. Small explosions from dozens of stories up send booming echoes that reverberate off skyscrapers covered with neon billboards—each explosion's pressure waves reach the crowd a fraction of a second before the sound. Store owners, in the market every day because their livelihood depends on sales, carry on as if the explosions don't exist; their nervous systems brace for the sound after the warning pressure change rolls through their body. Some of the shoppers, braving the danger for necessities for the first time since the initial series of attacks, jump, clutch their chests, and look around for confirmation that the sound affects others as much as it does them. Others maintain their stoic nonchalance.

The Operator keeps his head down and eyes forward, with no thoughts wasted on his fate as he walks through the market looking for a new broom for the pool hall.

Areas of the market are still demolished from where wreckage fell from the sky during the initial hovercraft slaughter. To the Operator's surprise, the sellers who didn't lose their stalls help their affected neighbors rebuild until someone visiting their own store pulls them away. It's a remarkable display of community from vendors who would have loved less competition before Jirasek's massive ship parked itself over the city and its minion ships cleared all air traffic by force. A competitor going out of business because of market forces is acceptable—it's fate, and speaks to the surviving vendor's quality. A random vehicle falling from the sky and taking out the competition is luck, and in another timeline the situation could be reversed. And so, sellers help each other rebuild, hoping generosity gains them more customers so their rivals will go out of business due to more organic reasons.

The large blue-green ovoid ship looming over the city straddles the Gamma and Sigma districts. The district designation doesn't matter above the third-level reclaimers that purify the air for the upper levels, where traveling throughout the city used to be as easy as hopping onto a hovercraft and flying to your destination. Before every flying vehicle became a target. Below the reclaimers, however, ancient barricades made of decomposing land-traveling cars and various other scrap metal keep the different districts' residents separate from each other, and each from Theta as well. The districts each have their own preferred distinguishing physical characteristic—Gamma's blue eyes, Sigma's pointed teeth, and Theta's clipped nostrils. The ship looks down on the city without regard for the consternation of the millions living above the reclaimers who believe they deserve better.

Another boom rings out, louder and closer than the rest, pulling the majority of eyes towards the sky. Unfazed, the Operator slides through the petrified crowd, weaving his way through the masses until he arrives at his destination. It shares its fabric walls with a jewelry store on one side and an artist's shop on the other, none of them yet affected by hovercraft debris. The stall he arrives in specializes in washing clothes but sells soaps and other cleaning supplies used by the pool hall. The owner, a bent-over lady with arthritis-ravaged joints, doesn't move from her chair when the Operator steps into her stall.

"Has it been a month already?" she asks, her lips curled in disgust. Her blue eyes watch the Operator's every move as if anything not bolted down could disappear along with the customer.

"No, it hasn't. We need a broom."

"Miguel needs a broom? Why doesn't he come himself?" she says, disappointed.

"He's busy keeping an eye on the pool hall." In truth, the fact that the old woman makes frequent sexual jokes to Miguel is the reason that he handed off responsibility for visiting her to the Operator in the first place.

"Well, tell him I miss him," the vendor says, her voice silk. She reaches over, grabs a gnarled cane, stands up, and readopts her disdain. "Are you going to need the usual order?"

"No, just a broom."

She walks over to a corner closet without taking her eyes from her customer, opens it, and pulls one out. Handing it over, she says, "I could come over there and help you sweep. One of *many* services I offer." Realizing who she's talking to, she adds, "For Miguel, not for you."

"I know," he says. He hands over a small white disk. "It's full. Just put the rest on our account."

The arthritic vendor's eyes open wide and she nods, tucking it into her bra for safekeeping. "Tell Miguel to come back next time," she says, backing up to her perch.

The Operator doesn't say anything and walks out of the stall.

There's yelling on the far side of the market as something

falls from the sky. After a loud crash, dozens of curious shoppers make their way towards the commotion—one of the hovercrafts braved the imposed ban on air traffic and didn't make it past the blockade. The ship above the city uses dozens of small sentinel ships to maintain the empty skies, all controlled by artificial intelligence. Ever since they ground city traffic to a halt, the city's population looks down on all nonorganic intelligence, androids included. The Operator is an advanced model and would be otherwise indistinguishable from the rest of the humans in the market, but his reputation means everyone knows who, and what, he is. To the city's residents, where the intelligence resides doesn't matter—ship or humanoid body, they're all at fault.

The ships all belong to Felipe Jirasek, owner and founder of Jirasek Industries, the largest manufacturer in the city. They make everything from hovercrafts to buildings, and once Jirasek saw the opportunity to take control of the entire city, and therefore the market, and drive all of his competitors out of business, he took it, launching his ship and making sure nothing but his own approved traffic travels through the skies. Rumors abound about him, some in praise, others cursing his name, but they all agree on one thing—he's the smartest person in the city, and his thirst for control puts everyone's future in question.

A woman with a small child's hand in her own brushes the Operator's arm in her rush towards the crash site. The child's tiny legs churn while keeping up with her pace, and in his haste he drops a small stuffed toy at the Operator's feet. The boy plants his feet, reaching with his other arm; his panicked screams are lost in the noise.

The Operator, broom in hand, reaches down and picks up the toy. It's a stuffed horse, with one eye missing, and filthy from frequent use. Looking in the direction the woman and her child went, he catches sight of them disappearing into the crowd.

Sighing, he starts towards the crash site as well, pushing his way through the masses. Several times a person he jostles past raises their voice at him and stands tall, and each time they shrink back when they realize who shoved them out of the way. When the crowd becomes too dense for continued progress, he scans the visible heads, looking for the mother.

He finds her three people ahead and off to his right. There's a fire raging ahead demanding everyone's attention, but it doesn't concern him. Pushing through the people between them, he reaches the woman, who has a vice grip on her child. Kneeling down, he hands the stuffed horse to her kid.

"What do you think you're doing?" the mother exclaims when she sees the Operator next to her son.

"He dropped this," the Operator says, standing back up.

"You took my son's toy!"

"No, I'm just giving it back. You weren't paying attention."

"Don't tell me how to mother my own child, *android*. You don't know the first thing about organics."

A murmur erupts from those around them once the accusation leaves her lips. All of a sudden, the Operator finds himself separated from everyone else by a wide margin, all of them staring at him as if he'll explode when provoked.

"Thank you," the boy says, hugging his toy.

"Don't mention it, kid," the Operator replies.

The mother picks her son up and faces the Operator with a scowl on her face. When her child turns his head around, she forces it back to the wreckage at her back.

The Operator turns around and walks away through the growing crowd, a space opening up around him as he walks, as if getting close to him is a vote in favor of Jirasek's aggression. He reminds himself not to worry about what they think as he walks all the way through Gamma's market, past the stares from the shopkeepers annoyed at the distraction pulling customers from their shopping. One vendor calls out to the Operator, asking, "What's going on over there?" before realizing who he is talking to and pretending he has other, more pressing matters somewhere in his shop.

Past the market, in the city streets built for vehicular traffic that now host pedestrians, the Operator exhales, grateful the crowds are behind him. Now that he's alone, he casts a quick glance overhead and sees the same sight that's been there for almost a week—the bottom of a massive ship, blocking what little light entered the city from the sun. Days and nights blend together under the flashing lights from the numerous neon billboards advertising everything from network solutions to toothpaste. Most, if not all, of the companies are no longer relevant because they can't get their products out to their consumers— the ones who still operate are under Jirasek's umbrella of companies. If the industrialist has his way, the rest of them will become his too, or they will be forced out because of his own backed competitor.

A rustle in the alley off to his right pulls the Operator's focus back to the ground. There are three men, their back to the Operator, surrounding a fourth young man. "Just give us the money and we'll leave you alone."

"I can't. We need this for food," the young man says. He grabs the small bag hanging from his necklace and puts it through his collar before clutching it beneath his shirt.

"Now why'd you have to go and do that?" the man on the right says. He's short, slender, and doesn't look like he's worth much in a fight. On the other hand, both of his companions are massive. One looks like he's a boy stretched to the size of a large man, with red hair in a bowl cut and a red-and-white-striped shirt. The other, a girl, has the largest shoulders of the group. From the way she's standing, the Operator sees her scowl and is impressed with its ferocity.

Something about the Operator's momentary pause pulls the victim's attention past the immediate threat and to the man standing on the sidewalk. "Hey! Help! They're trying to rob me!"

The three attackers turn and look at the Operator. The man in charge pulls out a blaster, which draws worried glances from both his comrades.

The Operator raises his hands. "Not my problem," he says, before continuing back to the pool hall.

In the background, the Operator hears a muffled yell, followed by a series of grunts and body blows. Whimpering reaches him between footsteps.

"Hey!" the leader calls from behind. There's a block between him and the muggers.

The Operator keeps walking at his measured cadence despite the rapid footsteps that originate from the alley. He stops and turns around when they get close. "You don't want to do this," he says.

A red flush creeps up the girl's neck and face. "What do you know about what we want to do?"

"Quiet, Arlecks, leave the talking to me," the leader spits. He turns to the Operator. "What do you know about what we want to do?" he says.

"Look, I'm just going home."

"Give me all your money and you can," the leader says. Numerous scars cover his face, creating spaces where hair doesn't grow in his eyebrows.

The leader brandishes his weapon and steps forward. "Don't make me use this. Hand it over."

"Can't do that," the Operator says, clutching the broom at his side with his left hand.

"What are you going to do with that? Sweep us off the street?" the leader says. Both his cronies laugh.

"Nope, just have some sweeping to do at home."

"Hand over your money and you can go take care of it!"

The Operator sighs and rolls his eyes. "No."

The leader steps forward and puts the blaster right in the Operator's face. With his other hand, he grabs the Operator's shirt. "Now, don't make me—"

Before the mugger can finish his threat, the Operator punches him in the solar plexus while ducking. The resulting shot flies over his head. He reaches up and grabs the gun while turning, throwing the broom between the girl's legs when she steps forward. She falls to the ground with a loud thud. The man-child is staring down the barrel of a blaster before he can even move towards the Operator, while the girl stares at a wrist bent at an odd angle and the leader wheezes from a kneeling position.

Incapacitating the group takes mere seconds.

"Wasn't my problem, until you made it my problem," the Operator says. He pulls another blaster from a hidden holster in his waistband on his back and compares the two weapons. His own blaster is jet black and seems to absorb light, with an impressive array of attachments. The seized weapon is a basic model, dingy silver covered with dents. Six eyes all stare at him with a mixture of anger and awe.

"You don't mind if I keep this one, do you? It's cheap, but good enough in a pinch."

The leader shakes his head. Following his lead, his two cronies also agree.

"Good." He reaches down and searches the leader's pockets, taking the stolen money before walking back to the pool hall and leaving the scavengers behind.

CHAPTER TWO

The Operator and Miguel look around the pool hall, Miguel's hands on his hips and the Operator's hand resting on the standing broom. The clean floor, spotless pool tables, and wall of cue sticks all wait for the night's guests. The few scratches on the green felt atop the tables left over from beginners are the sole evidence of the hall's frequent traffic—otherwise, tonight could be its grand opening.

After the most recent demolition of the establishment, which occurred when both Miguel and the Operator were away from the premises, the pair decided to do away with the previous decor. Cinder block walls replace where ancient posters and newspapers once hung. The pair ripped down the ancient ceiling, leaving the wires that run to the lights hanging over each pool table exposed. The change inspired visits from a new clientele—hard-drinking men that have no room or desire for anything pretentious or antiquated. Business rides on the back of the copious alcohol and Serum sales, earning Miguel—and by extension, the Operator—mountains of goodwill from the White Jackets, who make the Serum from whatever exhaled Stim the reclaimers pull from the air.

Serum perks up whoever drinks it but doesn't have the same addictive quality as Stim. Most people receive a slight boost to their energy from Serum, allowing them to stay engaged and active for longer than they would without. The drink gives the men who frequent the pool hall the energy and tolerance for long hours of drinking alcohol—their night always ends when the men get physical.

Breaking up fights at the pool hall gives the Operator plenty of practice with the hand-to-hand combat skills he learned from the Sect during his time in the badlands and unlocked during his fight with the now-dead Butler, the infamous two-gunned android. His reputation for fighting preserves for him the respect of the hardened men who visit the pool hall, and every single one gives him a slight nod when they enter, knowing full well it could be them who is on the receiving end of his blows, depending on how the night plays out. The Operator often wonders what would happen if any of the men took Stim before coming to the pool hall, or during their visit, and if he could still take control of the situation. He considers himself lucky that Gamma district went without Stim for so long during Bacas's reign that everyone now prefers a steady diet of Serum.

The night's first arrival is a sour-looking middle-aged man with sparse red hairs hanging from his chin. "Evenin', gentlemen," he says when he walks in.

"Evenin'," Miguel says. The Operator doesn't say a word, and hasn't since Jirasek's stunt put inorganic intelligence at the bottom of the totem pole. Not that he minds—it keeps him from wasting time talking to people while he scans the room for unrest.

"Who's comin' tonight?" Miguel asks. The same question he asks right after the man walks in every night.

"The usual." The same answer.

Despite seeing the typical men multiple nights a week, for

weeks on end, none of them bother with names. Miguel swears it's part of the reason why they keep coming back, and so he never breaks the streak. "It's part of the new atmosphere," he says as justification to the Operator when they're alone.

The man orders a Serum and a shot, taking both glasses from the bar and setting them down near his preferred table. The Operator has watched him win against every man that comes in, some multiple times, and it's a rite of passage for regulars—he won't accept a match until he's seen the same face for numerous nights.

More men stream in over the next hour until people are waiting for subsequent games around each table. Most of the men know the Operator is an android because of his various escapades in the city since he came back from the badlands. After their initial nod of recognition, they keep their distance for the rest of the night, until the moment when alcohol impairs their judgement and Serum perks them up and their true beliefs emerge. Then, some might sling a slur his way, calling him a robot, or talk about how machines aren't anything more than spare parts loud enough for everyone in the room to hear.

Once the night gets into the usual flow, Miguel plants himself behind the bar and provides a steady stream of liquids to the men. The Operator moves around, standing near the rowdiest customers despite their venomous glances.

"You cheated!" a stocky, gray-haired man says to the one with the sparse red chin hairs after the eight ball finds a corner pocket, cementing his loss. It's the first time they've played—the stocky man first started coming the previous week, brought by another regular.

The accused man stands tall and looks his accuser in the face. "Pick your next words carefully, friend."

The Operator steps closer to the malcontent.

"I'm not your friend! You double-tapped the cue ball. I saw

it move."

The winner looks around the table, waiting for potential corroborators. He holds his hand out to the left and the man holding the money hands over his winnings. "You're seeing things, pal. You're lucky I even played a punk like you—can't even take his loss like a man."

The Operator knows those words won't dissipate without retaliation. The stocky man grabs his cue stick and grips the thicker portion with both hands. "You're not going to steal my money . . ." he says as he takes a decisive step forward.

The winning player, seeing the Operator behind the aggressive man, doesn't move or blink.

Before the man can complete his swing, the Operator has his hands on the drawn-back cue stick.

"What the—"

The Operator rips the cue stick from the man's hands in one swift pull.

Enraged, the loser launches himself at the Operator, who steps to the side and uses the man's momentum against him. The man lands sprawled out on the floor. His embarrassment adds to his rage and he stands up for another attack. He positions both fists in front of his face and steps forward on his toes.

The Operator looks at Miguel. The pool hall's owner squeezes his lips together and shrugs, telling his friend to "do what you have to do," without uttering a word.

The attacker approaches the Operator, who has his hands at his side, and jabs with his left, a weak distraction for the powerful right-handed haymaker coming in from the other arm.

Seeing the coming strikes as if they're in slow motion, the Operator pulls his head back from the jab, then tilts to his right while at the same time deflecting the right-handed swing with his own left forearm. Then, he unleashes a devastating strike to the man's ribs with his right fist before standing tall.

The attacker's hip slams into the side of the next table with a thud, his torso coming to rest on the green felt. He grabs the cue ball with his left hand and stands back up, favoring his right side.

Everyone in the pool hall pays close attention to the ongoing fight. A man at the bar turns around and leans against the bar with his glass of Serum in hand, enjoying the spectacle.

"You don't want to do this," the Operator says.

"Just take your blaster out and be done with it," the game's winner says. "Who's got next?" he says, looking around. The rest of the men at his table laugh.

"Don't need it," the Operator replies.

The wounded attacker looks at the Operator's hip. Not seeing a holster, he roars and charges forward. This time, instead of waiting and using the man's momentum against him, the Operator steps forward, meeting the aggressor sooner than expected and rendering the wielded cue ball useless. The Operator wraps his arms around the man's torso, then turns around him and takes his back. His arms slide up and he puts the stocky man into a full nelson hold. The man reeks of alcohol.

"Drop the cue ball," the Operator growls in the man's ear.

"Go to hell!"

The Operator looks at the closest player, who reaches up and takes the cue ball while meeting minimal resistance. Then, the Operator escorts him outside, throwing him onto the sidewalk in a heap.

"You can come back tomorrow and win your money back. Don't drink so much and you might have a chance."

A sudden explosion overhead pulls the Operator's attention towards the sky. Countless bursts of fire illuminate the night, reflecting off the underside of the ship. It's too dark to know exactly what's going on, but the Operator guesses the city forces are taking action against Jirasek's ship. Again. And it doesn't look like they're even getting close enough to matter.

The man the Operator escorted out takes the opportunity afforded him by the distraction and launches himself at the Operator's midsection.

His attention pulled back to the ground by the sudden movement, the Operator lifts his knee and lands a savage strike to the man's face, knocking him out cold.

Every table is back in action when the Operator walks back inside, as if there had never been a distraction. The Operator goes to the bar and accepts a glass of Serum from Miguel, downing it in one long drink.

"He never stood a chance," Miguel says while wiping a glass with a white rag.

"City's going after Jirasek's ship again," the Operator says while he puts his glass back down on the bar.

"And?"

"Looks as fruitless as ever."

The first arrival hollers over to the Operator. "We've heard about that fancy shooting but never get to see it in action!" He has a slim lead over his next opponent and is waiting for his next turn.

"And you won't," the Operator replies.

"We'll see about that," the pool shark says with a wink. His opponent misses their shot and he's called into action once more.

The rest of the night passes by without any incident approaching the severity of the earlier fight. After the reminder about the Operator's fighting prowess, anyone who exchanges harsh words with another just has to spot the looming figure and they shut their mouths. There's a good chance one of them will forget the display the following day, and he's ready to remind them if they do.

Miguel often leans a single elbow on the bar while he watches the pool hall patrons with pride. Both elbows resting on the bar means he's exhausted, and the night's festivities should draw to a close. He'd never outright say it, but the Operator knows, and says it for him when it occurs.

"Finish up your games and get out! Closing time!" the Operator yells.

Miguel stands up with a start. "Are you sure?" he says to the Operator, always playing the friend to his clients.

The Operator doesn't mind being the bad guy. "Yes, I'm sure. We're tired, and we still have to clean up!"

"Do you even need to sleep?" one of the drunker men says. His face is flushed, and he has a smile pasted on his face.

His friend hits him in the arm.

"What'd you do that for?" he says, rubbing the sore spot.

"Let's just go," the friend says.

"All right, let me finish my drink." He downs the last remnants of Serum and together they stumble out. The rest of the men soon follow.

"Another killer night," Miguel says, setting the counted money back into the antique cash register when the pair are alone in the pool hall. "I'm spent—I'm heading to bed. Do whatever you want tonight and I'll get the rest tomorrow."

"'Night," the Operator says, grabbing his broom. He walks over to the front door and locks it before sweeping in his usual pattern, starting at the front and working his way to the back. He's getting into a groove when a loud thud from the front door startles him. Turning towards it, he sees the man he fought earlier trying to get back in—with a blaster in his hand.

"You broke my nose!" the man yells through the door. He bangs on the glass with the butt of his gun, breaking it after his third strike. Then, he sticks the gun through the created hole, seeking the Operator.

Frustrated, tired, and not in the mood, the Operator dives and rolls to his right, closing the distance between himself and the door. As he stands up, he pulls out his blaster and aims it at the wobbling arm. A long exhale centers him, and he tucks the blaster back into his rear waistband while walking towards the front door.

The man outside tries bending his arm and aiming at the Operator but his movements are delayed from too much drink. Before he can get the right angle, the Operator seizes his wrist and rips the gun from his hand.

For a second, the Operator thinks about breaking the man's arm. Instead, he yanks, pulling the man against the door and knocking him out once more. He takes the man's blaster—another cheap specimen—walks behind the bar, and adds it to the collected pile. Then, he starts sweeping all over again.

After sweeping the main room, the Operator stands next to the trash can behind the bar. He collects the pile of dust and debris, puts it inside the trash, and empties the receptacle, placing a new liner in the can. After leaning the broom against the bar, he walks out the back door and throws the bag into the dumpster.

"Ugh—" A grunt from inside.

"You can't sleep in there," the exasperated Operator says, peering over the dumpster's edge. In the faint light thrown by the neon billboards high above, he sees a person with short hair covered in black soot, the trash bag sitting atop their face.

They turn to their side and clutch their stomach.

The Operator reaches in and moves the trash bag before grabbing their shoulder and turning them so they're faceup. To his surprise, it's a woman. Her eyes flicker open, the whites just visible in the darkness, and she utters one word before passing out: "Help."

CHAPTER THREE

A SPOTLIGHT on a slow-moving hovercraft overhead passes perpendicular across the alley, further illuminating the woman in the dumpster. Her sleek crimson jumpsuit is in burned tatters.

The Operator realizes she doesn't have the blue sclerae typical in Gamma.

Hovercraft searches aren't a common sight below the reclaimers, and none would move so slowly when every flying craft has been shot out of the sky by Jirasek's fleet. Deciding that the hovercraft belongs to the man laying siege to the city, and that the industrialist must want this woman found for some reason, the Operator reaches into the dumpster—resting his hip on the metal edge—and grabs the woman's arm. She's unconscious and doesn't provide any help as he lifts her halfway out and slings her over the edge of the dumpster. The Operator prepares for the final effort by standing tall and cracking his back.

The spotlight reappears at the end of the alley and begins making its way between the two buildings.

"Great," the Operator says. After dealing with the population's condescending attitude towards inorganic intelligence because of Jirasek, helping his hovercraft find its target isn't high on his list of priorities.

He takes a moment and gauges the spotlight's speed, deciding if he can cover the distance between the dumpster and the pool hall's back door before they illuminate him. Unsure, he pushes the woman back into the dumpster and climbs in after her so the hovercraft has no reason for further investigation. Rats scramble out from under their combined weight. Once they're both inside the dumpster, he covers both of them with bags of trash.

With uncomfortable clarity, the Operator remembers that the last time he was this close to a woman was when he lay next to his then-fiancé and they both lived on the fifty-second level. Before he found out she was an android and left her behind and went to the badlands. When he still didn't know that he was an android himself.

The spotlight stops above the dumpster, throwing blinding light onto the trash covering the two hidden bodies. The Operator repositions his head so he can see the vehicle above, but the light blinds him. The rancid smell of rotting food fills his nostrils, and he feels movement as rats survey the visitor in their domain. After tense seconds pass, the spotlight moves on. When it does, the Operator sees the trailing bottom of the ship in the retreating light—a dark blue-green metal ovoid, the same sentinel type that's been shooting down every flying ship in the city.

The Operator rushes into action before the spotlight can double back—or another one comes along—throwing the trash off himself and the woman. Setting his feet on the shifting bags, he lifts the woman out halfway, again resting her on the dumpster's edge. Then, he climbs out before lifting her the rest of the way. Holding on to her torso from beneath her armpits, he walks backwards back into the pool hall and shuts the door behind them.

"Miguel!" the Operator calls out.

No response.

The Operator leaves the woman in a pile just inside the back door and walks to Miguel's room. He opens the door, casting a sliver of light over the upper half of the bed within. Miguel looks at him and turns his back to the intrusion.

"Get up," the Operator says, turning on the room's light.

"I just fell asleep," Miguel grumbles.

"We have a visitor."

"Tell them we're closed."

"It's a woman. Jirasek's looking for her."

The mention of Jirasek is a splash of cold water. Miguel sits up and looks at the Operator, squinting in the light.

"How do you know that?" he asks.

"Hovercraft was looking for her. Nobody can fly in the city without Jirasek's permission without being shot down. It had to be them."

"What do they want with someone this far down?"

"Beats me. But she's in bad shape."

Miguel stands up wearing just his underwear and puts on a pair of shorts before following the Operator to the back door.

The woman's arm is at an odd angle beneath her body, and her legs are in a tangle. Miguel rearranges her so she's lying flat on her back, her arms at her side.

Seeing her in the light, with her face relaxed and chest rising and falling with ragged breaths, the Operator can't help but think she looks like his former fiancée—though he can't decide if it's because he already had Patrice on his mind when they were together in the dumpster. It's a name he hasn't thought of for a long time, and focusing on the sensation of shaking his head helps clear the unwanted memory from his mind.

Miguel and the Operator stand shoulder to shoulder, looking down at the soot-covered woman.

"What should we do with her?" Miguel asks.

"Beats me. Think she'll wake up?"

"We could always go get the healer . . ." Miguel had spent many nights with the famed healer at her facility on the line between Sigma and Gamma, but the relationship cooled when the pool hall's consistent business made traveling to her impossible—she never left her plants alone for the night. He's been looking for an excuse to see her ever since.

"We can tomorrow, if she doesn't show any signs of recovering," the Operator says.

"Well, how about you head to bed and I'll clean her up," Miguel offers.

The Operator looks at him with mild disgust.

"It's not like that! We can't just leave her filthy, and there's no reason for both of us to do it." Miguel walks back to his room and the Operator goes into his own, which also doubles as storage. Before shutting his door, the Operator sees Miguel walk past with an old shirt and pants. He gives the pool hall owner a look.

"All business," Miguel says, his jaw set.

Thirsty when he wakes up, the Operator leaves the storage room and walks into the pool hall's main area, shirtless and wearing his black pants. He fills a glass of water from the tap and takes a long drink. Looking into the rest of the room with his mouth full of water, he almost spits it out when he sees the woman from the dumpster lying on the closest pool table, remembering the events from the night before. Miguel's clothes hang off of her, and her hands are folded over her chest. Her breathing, shallow and ragged before he went to sleep, is now steady.

"She seems to be getting better," Miguel says from where the pool hall meets the back hallway. His eyes are bloodshot, with dark circles beneath.

"You look terrible," the Operator tells him.

"No worse than you," Miguel says, his retort hollow.

"Guess we won't need the healer," the Operator says.

"I still might go visit," Miguel says with a twinkle in his eye. "I was up all night making sure she didn't take a turn for the worse."

"I can tell. Why don't you get some sleep; I'll go to the market and get some clothes that fit her."

Miguel nods. "We might have to keep the place closed tonight if she doesn't wake up."

"We could just keep her in your bed," the Operator suggests.

"We could . . . but I don't want her waking up and walking out into here when it's filled with people. We're busy enough each night as it is and won't be able to deal with her."

"Fair point. Go get some rest, and I'll be back with new clothes for her."

Miguel shuffles back to his room and shuts the door. The Operator hears him collapse onto his bed while he puts on his black long-sleeved shirt and silver suspenders, then puts on his black boots and ties them. The silver belt and holster stay hanging from a nearby chair, his blaster instead tucked into his rear waistband. He walks past the woman on the pool table on his way out. "Don't wake up. I'll be back soon," he says, walking through the door with a fresh hole from the previous night's rowdy patron and shutting it behind him.

The woman is awake when the Operator returns. He

watches her through the hole in the door before he walks in; she's sitting on the edge of the pool table, looking around with curiosity. After making noise at the door so he won't surprise her, he opens it and walks into the pool hall.

She turns around and looks at him with large, alert eyes.

"Hello," the Operator says. He approaches the pool table she's sitting on and puts the clothes he bought at the market for her down next to her. "These are for you," he says.

The woman doesn't say a word. She leans over, looks into the bag, then looks back at the Operator.

"I'll go into the back so you can put them on," he says. When she looks like she understands, he walks back to the storage room, sits down on a box near where he sleeps, and waits.

Miguel's door opens and the tired man appears in the Operator's doorway. "Who are you talking to?" he asks.

"Our guest. She's awake."

Miguel perks up at the news. Before the Operator can stop him, he steps away from the storage room and goes into the main hall with the Operator close behind.

"She's—" the Operator says. He doesn't get the chance to finish his statement. Standing next to a pool table, the woman has on a tight black short-sleeved shirt, black pants, and black boots. Miguel's clothes are on the ground next to her.

"You couldn't get her anything with color?" Miguel says. "Not everyone likes all black."

The woman stands before the two men, brushes something from her leg, and smiles.

"I think she does," the Operator says, nodding towards the woman.

"What's your name?" Miguel asks the woman.

She stares at him in response. There's no attempt at

speaking—it's as if the concept of her own communication doesn't exist.

"Can you talk?" the Operator asks.

Her eyes swivel to the Operator, but still no response. The men could be noise machines making sounds in her direction and her reaction would be the same.

"Maybe she's mute?" Miguel says. Looking at her, he lifts his right hand to his mouth then splays his fingers as he pulls it away from his face.

"No, she definitely said 'help' last night."

"Maybe she's deaf?"

"Don't think that's it either—she looks at us when we talk."

"This is strange," Miguel says. He approaches the woman, looking at her face. She smiles.

"I say we stay closed tonight, until we can figure out what to do with her."

"Your call," the Operator says.

The afternoon passes while the pair try various forms of communication. They try different languages, gestures, and sounds, and none earn them more than inquisitive stares. The pool hall's typical first arrival shows up at his customary time, peeking through the hole in the door at the three individuals inside. "Are you going to let me in?" he yells out, his voice heavy with frustration at finding the door locked. The woman, now standing near the bar, looks at the source of the noise.

"Closed tonight, come back tomorrow," Miguel calls out in response.

"Closed? Come on, open up!"

"Closed! Because of your friend that caused trouble last night. If you've got a problem, take it up with him!" Miguel says.

"That punk better watch his back," the pool shark mutters, turning away.

Miguel and the Operator refocus their attention on the woman. Miguel brings out three steaming bowls of a thick porridge from the back. He eats in silence with the Operator while they stand at the bar—the woman doesn't touch her food despite the insistence of her companions but watches them eat. All of a sudden, someone bangs on the front door, and all three look towards the sound.

"I told you, we're closed!" Miguel yells, before realizing the face pressed against the intact piece of glass is the man who fought the Operator the night before. Standing behind him, his face contorted in anger, is the pool shark.

"Look. Look! Now we can't go in, because of you."

The Operator pulls his blaster from his rear waistband and approaches the front door. "All right, that's enough," he says, gesturing with the muzzle off to the side. He turns around, and instead of finding the woman's look of mild fascination, he comes face-to-face with cold, determined eyes.

"Your blaster," the woman says. Her voice is hoarse, out of practice.

Miguel stares at the woman with a spoonful of food hovering in front of his lips.

"My blaster," the Operator says, putting it behind his back and tucking it away.

"All you had to do was show it and they got the point?" she asks.

Miguel drops his spoon back into the bowl. "You speak!"

"I do, yes," the woman says, looking confused.

"What's your name?" Miguel asks.

"Lucy."

"Lucy . . . I'm Miguel, and this—"

"How did you get into the dumpster last night?" the Operator asks, cutting off his friend.

"Dumpster?"

"Yes, where I found you, before I brought you in here."

Lucy looks down at her boots, pants, and shirt, as if seeing them for the first time. She looks around at the pool hall, then Miguel, and finally the Operator. "I don't remember."

CHAPTER FOUR

——————————

LUCY DOESN'T REMEMBER anything other than her name. She has no recollection of where she came from, what she did before, or even her previous time spent in the pool hall. Seeing the Operator's blaster woke her up in a brand-new body, shocking her back to the present. The clothes she put on aren't what she would have chosen, she says, but she likes them.

"Makes me look intimidating," she says, standing up and adopting a ready stance, an imaginary blaster in her hand.

"Have you shot a blaster before?" Miguel asks.

"Looks like it," the Operator adds. He grabs one of the blasters from the collection behind the bar—a standard Enforcer weapon he can't remember adding to the pile—and hands it to her.

Lucy looks at the blaster with trepidation before grabbing it. Then, with a deft flick of her wrist, she examines the energy source within before positioning it at chest height and aiming down the sights at the front door.

"You've done this before," the Operator says.

Lucy stands tall, relaxes, and twirls the gun around her right index finger before miming putting the weapon into a holster at her waist. "Agreed."

"Let's go out back and see how good you are with that thing," the Operator says.

"Ahem," Miguel says, clearing his throat. He pushes the third bowl towards the woman, then looks at the Operator before looking at his half-eaten portion. "Eat first, then you can shoot."

Lucy looks at the Operator. "Does he always look out for you like this?" she jokes, setting the blaster on the bar.

"Only about food."

Lucy and the Operator stand in front of the bar, Miguel behind. The Operator and Lucy shovel their food down at an astonishing rate—Miguel's eating is further slowed compared to theirs when he stops and stares at their rapid spoonfuls. The Operator finishes first, since he had already eaten some from his bowl, but Lucy isn't far behind.

"All right, let's go see what you've got," the Operator says when they're done.

"And what, leave me to eat here by myself? Wait for me to finish; don't be rude."

The Operator and Lucy exchange a smile then turn towards Miguel. The pool hall owner, aware of the eyes trained on him, blows on his porridge despite it being room temperature, and takes a bite. After a second performative spoonful eaten in silence, he looks at the pair with frustration.

"Go on then, if you're just going to stare at me while I eat!"

The Operator laughs. Lucy follows his lead with an awkward chuckle.

"No, we'll wait," the Operator says.

"Then start talking so it's not so awkward," Miguel says, pushing flecks of food from the sides of the bowl into the main portion at the bottom.

"Well . . . I . . ." the Operator says, looking for traction.

"Tell her about yourself," Miguel says. "Did you know he spent time in the badlands?" he says to Lucy.

"What are the badlands?" Lucy asks, turning her attention to the Operator.

The Operator describes the dry, abandoned desert outside the city's limits, explaining how he went there after running away from his life on the upper levels. Lucy learns about his time with the Sect, meeting Fenix, and how the dog fell victim to Bacas upon his return to the city.

"Did he get away with it?" Lucy asks, her eyes wide.

"No. I came back and killed him. That's when I found out that I'm an android."

Lucy's eyes glaze over for a moment and the Operator wonders if he'll have to explain what an android is—she didn't know about the badlands, after all. After a moment, she comes back to the present with a shake of her head.

"You are? I couldn't even tell."

"Neither can most," Miguel says, dropping his spoon into an empty bowl. "That's the higher-level ones for ya, made to fit in with people. And a good thing too, now that Jirasek's little stunt put a target on their back."

"Do you ever have problems?" Lucy asks the Operator.

"People keep their distance," he says. He rearranges the spoon in his bowl.

"They can tell?"

"No, they just know what I've done around here. And word travels fast."

Lucy looks at the Operator with compassion, making him uncomfortable. He proposes they go outside before she can voice her sympathy. "Now that he's done," the Operator adds, nodding towards Miguel.

"Go on, I'll clean up," Miguel grumbles, gathering the

bowls. When he takes them to the back, the Operator leads Lucy around the bar and shows her his seized weapons. There are eleven blasters in total, ranging in size from ones that could fit in the palm of a hand to massive hand cannons and two blaster rifles.

"Why do you keep them behind the bar?" Lucy asks.

"Easy access when we might need them most," the Operator replies.

Lucy says she'll keep the one the Operator gave her in the first place and takes it from the bar. She follows the Operator out into the abandoned alley out back.

"Remember that?" the Operator says, pointing to the dumpster.

"No . . ."

"That's where I found you," the Operator says. He approaches the dumpster and selects a few pieces of trash—a broken glass, an old shoe, and three empty Serum bottles. "Stay here," he says, running down the alley with the three bottles in hand, leaving the broken glass and shoe behind. When he determines he's far enough from Lucy, he sets down the three bottles with two paces between each. Setting down the final bottle, he sees black, sootlike smudges he doesn't remember ever seeing before. He swears he can see handprints . . .

"What are you waiting for?" Lucy yells.

"I'm coming," the Operator replies, jogging back to her side.

"Okay, let's see what you've got," the Operator says. He expects Lucy will raise her blaster, take careful aim, and fire when she has the first bottle in sight.

Instead, Lucy stands still, with her legs shoulder width, the gun in her right hand hanging at her side. She exhales with her eyes closed. In a flash of movement, she brings both hands up to chest height in front of her, her left hand wraps around her right and the handle, and she fires as soon as the weapon is at the correct height.

The first bottle shatters in the distance, spraying glass and remaining droplets of Serum all over the cracked asphalt.

The Operator turns to Lucy with his eyes wide open. "You've shot before," he says.

"Looks like it." A moment later, she asks the Operator if he's going to shoot one.

"No," he says, laughing. "I want to see what you can do."

"Your loss," Lucy says. She stands still again with the blaster at her hip and exhales. A piece of paper blows by, caught in an air current. All of a sudden, she shifts her weight to her right leg, bends her right arm at a ninety-degree angle while bringing her left hand over and laying it atop both her right thumb and the gun barrel, and fires, all in one rapid motion. The second bottle disintegrates.

The Operator emits a loud whistle. "Getting fancy."

"Felt right."

"One left."

To the Operator's surprise, Lucy turns around and faces the opposite direction. She sets up the same way as before. This time, she turns to her left while reaching across her body with her right arm, firing from her hip with her shoulders square to the adjacent building. The shot finds its mark.

"She might be better than you," Miguel says with a chuckle from the doorway to the alley where he snuck up on the display. He turns around and goes back inside before the Operator can reply.

"Why'd you leave the upper levels in the first place?" Lucy asks, battling the descending silence. "You said you went to the badlands."

"There was someone who . . . she wasn't who I thought she was." In his mind's eye, he sees Patrice's father standing behind her, a small tool in his hand, playing in the circuits in the back of her skull. He didn't know she was an android at the time—and wouldn't find out he was one until many years later—and the shock inspired his rapid exit. Looking back isn't an option, and there's no room for regrets.

"Seems like you've done well for yourself down here," Lucy says while aiming down the sights in the direction of the broken bottles, pulling the Operator from his memories.

"That's one way of putting it," he says with a laugh. "Let's see what you can do with a moving target."

After grabbing the shoe, he stands a few paces away from Lucy and off to one side. She holds the blaster with both hands, pointed at the ground, and nods. He throws the shoe in the air as high as he can. Lucy brings the blaster up and hits the shoe twice—once the moment the shoe hung in the air before it changed direction because of gravity, and again when it skipped into the air after the first shot.

"Can you do that?" Lucy asks, turning her head to the perfect smug angle.

The Operator gives her a thin-lipped smile, his eyes closed. "Tell me when you throw it," he says before turning around.

On Lucy's call, the Operator swivels to his left and finds the thrown shoe in the air—she waited before her alert. Firing from his hip, he hits it once on the way up, then three more times as it skips in the air. Movement at the end of the alley distracts him before he can fire a fifth shot.

The shoe falls to the ground as the figure in the distance comes into focus. It's a man looking in their direction wearing dark glasses that cover the upper half of his face—an Enforcer.

Enforcers are notorious for not having a direct view of the world; instead, their Hololenses take in their surroundings and display them for the user, adding in lines for distance, illuminating dark corners, and providing data about important objects.

Bacas never used them because he never got his hands dirty; according to rumors, he was an outlier. They're standard issue and give the city's Enforcers an edge as they control the city's population.

"Let's go inside," the Operator says, extending his arm and ushering Lucy in before him. He shuts the door without giving the man at the end of the alley another glance.

"Done?" Miguel asks from the other room.

The Operator and Lucy walk into the main area of the pool hall. Miguel can tell something is wrong right away. "What is it?" he asks.

"Enforcer, at the end of the alley."

"All the way down here? Shouldn't they all be focused on getting rid of Jirasek? They have bigger fish to fry."

"I know, but there's one down here. Hololenses and everything."

Miguel's face scrunches up. "I wonder what they—"

Banging on the front door interrupts him. Wide black glasses perched on a bulbous nose riddled with acne scars appear in the hole in the door. "You going to invite us in?" they yell.

"We're closed for the night," the Operator yells back.

"Let me rephrase that: let us in or we're kicking down the door!"

The Operator looks at Miguel, who nods. Then, he walks over to the front door and lets in three large men, all of them with dark glasses covering their eyes.

"That's better," the first man says, standing tall and shrugging with self-importance. He scans the room. "That's her," he says to his comrades.

The two men with him rush towards Lucy. The Operator stands in their way and they pause. "What do you want with her?" he says.

"She's wanted by the higher-ups. You understand," the leader says while nodding towards Lucy.

One of the men closest to the Operator shoves him to the side. When he resists, they pull out their blasters.

The leader chimes in from behind. "This is a nice place. We can take the girl and go, or we can destroy it and take her when we're done."

The Operator looks at Miguel. The pool hall owner lowers his eyes and looks at the bar.

"Your choice," the leader says.

"Go on," the Operator replies. As he watches, the two Enforcer cronies grab a barstool and make Lucy sit on it. Then, the leader walks behind her and pulls a small tool from his pocket. He reaches up and moves Lucy's hair out of the way before pushing a button behind her left ear. Her eyes close as a small door in the back of her skull opens with a low hiss, exposing the wires behind.

Lucy is an android, just like him. Like Patrice. The Operator's stomach writhes and his hand twitches. His head jerks to the side, and he shakes it. He looks at Lucy again and their eyes meet.

In the next instant, the Operator withdraws his blaster and fires two quick shots, finding the heads of the two cronies. He stands tall and brings the blaster to chest height, aiming it at the leader before the man can withdraw his own weapon. The Enforcer pulls his glasses up, resting them on his head, as he backs away with his hands in the air.

"You don't want to do this," the man says, his voice stern.

"I don't?" the Operator replies.

"Why do you care? She's just an android . . ." His features harden, and his eyebrows pinch over his nose. "There's going to be so many Enforcers coming down on this—"

A shot from the Operator right between his eyes puts an end

to his speech. A trickle of blood creeps down his face before he falls.

As the Operator collects all three pairs of Hololenses, Miguel goes behind Lucy and closes her head. "No reason to have you exposed to the world," he says with a sheepish grin. Her eyes fly open.

Looking over the three bodies, Miguel remarks how cleaning up actual humans is trickier than cleaning up androids. "There's so many more fluids," he says with a grimace.

"How many times have you done this?" Lucy asks.

Just then, the trio hear the back door open. The Enforcer from the alley storms into the pool hall's main area, his blaster drawn, and comes face-to-face with the barrel of the Operator's.

"Too many," the Operator says, pulling the trigger.

CHAPTER FIVE

"We could just put them in the dumpster," Miguel suggests, his hands on his hips. The four bodies in the pool hall are stacked on top of trash bags behind the bar so that nobody looking into the establishment through the front door sees the carnage. The blood-covered rags the Operator, Lucy, and Miguel used when cleaning the floors form a pile on top of the uppermost corpse.

"Too close," the Operator grunts, cleaning blood from beneath his fingernails with a toothpick.

"We'll say someone put them there without us knowing," Miguel says.

"Do you really think they'll believe that?" Lucy asks. It's a genuine question, said without expected sarcasm.

Miguel thinks for a moment. "Doubt it," he says with a sigh, his shoulders sagging.

"Enforcers will be out for blood," the Operator says.

"Revenge," adds Lucy, as if she learned the word's definition a short while ago.

"Then where can we put them?" Miguel asks.

"I have an idea, but it's going to take all night."

The Operator and Lucy, each with a filled trash bag slung over their shoulder, take a series of back alleys to the train station. There, they hop down onto the tracks and walk into the midline's shadow. The sound of metal on metal reaches their ears from somewhere deep within.

"You sure nobody comes down here?" Lucy asks in a whisper.

"Nobody from the surface," the Operator says, less concerned with the volume of his voice. "Must have been a midliner."

"A midliner," Lucy says, weighing the word on her tongue.

It's the Operator's turn to whisper. "The people on the surface are scared of them. Nobody will find the bodies."

After a few more steps into the darkness, the Operator tells Lucy they've traveled far enough from the entrance. "Dump 'em," he says.

They both sling their cargo onto the ground and untie the bags. "Empty them onto the ground and leave the inner bag here—we'll take the outer bag back with us," the Operator says, referring to the double bag.

Walking back without their load takes half the time. When they get back to the pool hall, Miguel has a series of bags filled with body parts standing vertical, waiting for transport.

"We can reuse these," the Operator says, handing the outer bags to Miguel.

"Do you really think they'll eat the meat?" Miguel asks the Operator for what seems like the hundredth time.

"They eat rats—why would they care where their meat comes from?" the Operator says, repeating his earlier rationalization. "And if they don't, nobody ever goes into the midline."

The Operator's estimate for how long the process would take proves prescient. Lucy and he take their last trip in the hours before the first vendors show up at Gamma's market, a short distance from the entrance to the train station.

As they dump their last bit of cargo, a familiar voice reaches the Operator's ears.

"They said it was you," says Usryd from the shadows.

"Ran into trouble on the surface," the Operator replies to his old friend, pulling the extra trash bag through his hand and folding it in half.

"And so you decided to stink up our home with rotting meat?"

"It's not like that," the Operator replies. Lucy takes half a step closer to him.

"What's it like then?" Usryd asks. The dark shape of a human walking on all fours emerges in the shadows.

"We'll be killed if they find the bodies on the surface."

"Told you it was human!" another voice screeches from somewhere behind Usryd.

"And what will happen if they find the bodies on our doorstep? We don't want your problems!"

"I thought you could use . . ." the Operator says. He can't bring himself to finish the sentence.

"The meat? That we'd eat *humans*?"

"We're humans too, you know!" the second midliner voice says. "Typical surface-dweller, thinking you're better than us!"

The Operator hears Usryd's harsh whispering.

"I'd ask you to take the bodies back with you, but I know it's not possible."

The Operator waits in darkness. All of a sudden, he feels a hand on the small of his back. It surprises him because he didn't hear anyone approach.

Usryd's voice rings out strong and clear from below the Operator's shoulder. "Because of what you've done for me in the past, I'll make sure this problem disappears. But think twice before you show up here again—I can't guarantee you won't be attacked." Then, Usryd drops his voice to a whisper. "Sorry," he adds, patting the Operator's back twice.

"We appreciate it," Lucy says.

"And leave us out of the problems on the surface!" Usryd proclaims, his voice carrying down the abandoned tunnel.

"Noted," the Operator says. Turning to Lucy, he tells her it's time to leave. On the way back, he explains how Usryd helped him recover after a protracted interrogation session and how he saved Usryd's brother's life.

"So you two know each other," Lucy says with a chuckle.

The Operator doesn't respond.

Back in the pool hall, the Operator and Lucy tell Miguel about how the midliners were upset with their decision.

"What can they do, go to the Enforcers? They don't leave the midline," Miguel says, dismissing the pushback.

"Usryd was doing it for the others," the Operator says, resting his elbows on the bar.

"And what about the Hololenses?" Miguel says, picking up a trash bag and shaking it, rattling the electronics within.

The Operator stands straight up. "Why didn't you put them in the bags?" he says, exasperated. "Those are a dead giveaway the Enforcers were here."

"Well nobody will find them here, unless they have tracking chips—in which case, we're in for a world of trouble no matter what!" Miguel shoots back, setting the bag down.

"They can do that?" Lucy asks, staring at Miguel with wide eyes.

"Do you think—" says Miguel, looking at the Operator.

"No."

"But they could have—"

"Maybe that's how they found me," Lucy says, looking down at her shoes.

The trio become quiet while they think.

"I don't think you're tagged. If you were, they wouldn't have been out scouring the streets looking for you," the Operator says.

Lucy sighs, unconvinced.

"What if the Enforcers were tagged?" Miguel asks.

"Then the midliners will have some more guests very soon," the Operator replies without remorse. "At any rate, we need to get rid of the Hololenses. And find somewhere safe for her."

"Me?" says Lucy, pointing to herself.

"You can't stay here. There could be more Enforcers."

"And now you can't hide in the midline," says Miguel.

"I know," the Operator says, his voice giving away his frustration with both Miguel and the situation.

After a few moments, Miguel says, "Why don't you take her to the android refugee camp? She'd fit right in."

"No way. I'm not bringing this much heat over there. Cass would kill me."

"But—"

"I'm not doing it."

The Operator and Miguel both fall silent once more. Miguel leans against the bar counter with his arms crossed. "Well then, you have to ask her."

"It's looking like it."

"Ask who?" says Lucy.

Miguel and the Operator answer at the same time. "Klepsydra," says the Operator. "The White Jackets," Miguel says.

"Klepsydra's the leader of the White Jackets."

"She took over after he killed Bacas, the former Enforcer down here," Miguel explains.

"So she's the Enforcer now?"

"Not exactly—they won't make it official, and she's not happy about it," Miguel explains.

"I don't know if she'll do it," says the Operator.

"Why not?" asks Miguel.

"Why does she do anything?"

The matter settled, the Operator leaves the pool hall's main area and goes back into his room without another word. He takes a look around before putting on his silver belt and holster, cinching it tight around his waist. When the Operator and Lucy leave for Gamma's market, Miguel stays behind at the pool hall. If Enforcers do show up, he can say they asked questions and moved on. Otherwise, business as usual.

With the bag of electronics slung over his shoulder, the Operator walks with Lucy through Gamma's market to the smoking lounge that doubles as an entrance to the gang's hide-out. After telling the man running the stall their purpose, the Operator and Lucy are led through a series of corridors until they emerge in an abandoned theater. A table surrounded by mismatched chairs sits front and center on the stage.

"Sit here and I'll find her," the man says, walking through the dusty curtains hanging down from the rafters.

"Can anyone just ask to see her?" Lucy asks as the pair sit down.

"No. That guy knows me—we've fought before," the Operator says, leaning back in his chair and resting a hand on the table.

They don't have to wait long. They hear Klepsydra yelling before she appears. "If you're here, who's watching the stall?"

The man who led them up runs from the back, jumps off the stage, and sprints through the rows of seats before disappearing. A moment later, Klepsydra walks from the back with two women following close behind. All three have bright blue eyes and wear White Jackets, remnants from how the gang got their name in the first place—the foot soldiers no longer bother with the clothing, preferring their true allegiance hidden. Everyone in Gamma still knows who works for who despite their best efforts at secrecy.

"What do you want?" Klepsydra says to the Operator, the bird tattoo on her neck moving as she speaks. She pulls the chair at the head of the table out and sits down. Her two attendants stand behind her.

"We need help."

"Of course you do."

"I've got a gift for you," the Operator says, putting the bag with the four pairs of Hololenses onto the table and withdrawing the contents.

Klepsydra whistles. "Do I even want to know where you got these?" she asks, picking a pair up.

"No."

"I take it the tracking is disabled?"

The Operator shifts in his seat. "Tracking?"

"You led them straight here!" Klepsydra says, tossing the Hololenses back onto the table like they're red-hot coals.

"Aren't you the Enforcer for Gamma?" Lucy asks.

"And who are you?"

"Lucy."

Klepsydra turns to the Operator. "She your girlfriend?" she asks with a sneer.

"No."

Klepsydra then breaks into a broad smile. "There's no tracking—no Enforcer in the city would agree to being tracked like that," she says with a laugh, picking up the pair once more. She puffs up her chest and sticks her elbows out. "I'm the law, nobody tracks me," she says, her voice deep, pretending she's a man.

The Operator exhales.

"Okay, four Hololenses. What do you want?"

"We need somewhere for her to hide."

Klepsydra measures Lucy with her eyes. "Am I correct in assuming this has something to do with the Hololenses?"

"Do you really want to know?"

"No, but now I want to guess." She looks at the Hololenses on the table. "Four Enforcers showed up at your buddy's pool hall, searching for her. For some reason, you thought it would be a good idea to get rid of them instead of letting them take her."

Klepsydra pauses for a moment then stands up. She continues while walking around the table. "You found somewhere for the bodies, knowing there was no way in hell I'd have anything to do with that, and thought you could buy some goodwill with their Hololenses." She turns and looks at the Operator. "How am I doing so far?"

The Operator doesn't move a muscle.

"Now, before I go on, I do want to tell you a little secret—I can't stand the Enforcers. We work together, but do you know how many replacements I've had to get rid of?" She looks at her two cronies and laughs. "At this point you'd think they'd learn to just make me the one in charge!" She turns back to the Operator. "You can bet that I wouldn't have let you get the jump on me."

Lucy sits taller in her chair. The Operator stares at Klepsydra with cold eyes and asks the gang's leader if she's done.

"For now," Klepsydra says, sitting back down at the head of the table. "So, what exactly do you want? The Gamma residents aren't going to be happy I'm helping you if they ever find out— I've had more requests to get rid of the 'android filth' than I can count."

"Like I said, we need somewhere for her to hide," the Operator says, ignoring the insult. "And I want to know if and when Enforcers are coming back down below the reclaimers—I don't want to be surprised again."

"Ah. Now there's an interesting question—I'd like to know

when they come down too! As annoyed as you were at their arrival, which they found out the hard way, I'm also annoyed that they think they can walk into my district without saying a word to me."

The Operator stays silent.

"I'll tell you if I manage to find out, and you can take care of them for me."

"And hiding her?"

"We can help with that too, but it's going to take more than a few pairs of Hololenses."

"I had a feeling you were going to say that," the Operator says, taking a big breath while he stares at a grinning Klepsydra. "What do you want?"

"How familiar are you with the border between Gamma and Sigma?"

CHAPTER SIX

THE OPERATOR kicks a cylindrical piece of metal sitting on the cracked pavement that runs through Gamma, the same one he came in on from the badlands. The metal is heavier than expected and sends a jolt through his leg. Instead of skittering down the road, it turns over twice and comes to rest on the ground with a thud. Thankful for his boots, the Operator takes a few wary steps while noticing the sensations in his foot. He stops and takes a big step forward with the opposite leg, leaving the back leg in place and lifting his heel, feeling all of his toes.

Convinced his foot isn't damaged, he continues on to the barrier between Gamma and Sigma. When he gets to the ancient, rusted barrier made of old cars and scrap metal, he turns around and surveys the area. The buildings on each side of the street rise all the way to the highest levels of the city. Above the reclaimers, flashing advertisements in a range of neon colors light up the early morning. The walls below the reclaimers are descending into decrepitude—entire sections covered in sheets of plastic, large holes in ground-level walls, broken glass inside window openings, and layers of graffiti faded from years of exposure to the persistent haze.

GOOD ENOUGH IN A PINCH

"Don't believe what they look like from the outside for a second," Klepsydra had warned him. "They're doing just fine. And they haven't paid district taxes in months."

The Operator starts on the left side of the street. He walks to the entrance closest to the barrier, a wooden door with thick seams of space where the material rotted away. After knocking twice, he takes out his blaster and holds it in his right hand while pushing the door open with his left.

There's nobody inside. A filthy, decaying mattress and colorless food wrappers cover the ground, and a thick layer of dust sits atop everything in the space. There's a light from somewhere deep within that illuminates part of the hall extending from the front room. The Operator continues through the space, wondering about the type of people he's collecting taxes from and how they've managed eluding the White Jackets for so long. Klepsydra's words echo in his head. "We were going to send our own team, but why don't you just do it for us—in exchange for her protection."

The Operator turns right into a long-abandoned kitchen at the end of the hall. There's a space where a refrigerator once sat, and the walls around the stove are covered in black burn marks. The table in the center sits at an angle because of a broken leg. Black lumps sit on a plate on the counter, former food well past hosting mold or emitting a rancid smell. Tendrils of light shine through the barricaded window and door at the back. Putting his face to the cracks, the Operator peers through clear plastic into a blurred garden oasis in the courtyard.

Green plants cover every surface. There are rows of shoulder-height plants in the center, each one sitting inside a white bucket and reaching to an unseen light source high above. Leaning down and angling his gaze up, the Operator sees sheets of clear plastic also cover the overhead space. Building the space and keeping it operational takes money—money that hasn't been taxed.

Instead of pulling down the barricade and tearing through the plastic, the Operator leaves the dilapidated property behind and proceeds to the next entrance on the block, knowing he'll find whoever has access to the courtyard as he works his way around the building. The door leading inside is in the same condition as the previous one, except there's black material on the back side and it doesn't budge when pushed. Deciding against knocking, he kicks the door down; it slams open, cushioned by blankets from hitting the wall behind. The Operator finds himself staring into a residence cared for by someone fighting against time. The dark wood floors, covered with scuff marks and deep scratches, are swept clean, and a layer of brown stains covers the once-white walls. There are handprints at waist height.

"Mom!" a child yells, their feet pattering away into the depths of the residence. The Operator, his blaster in hand, walks through the door at the far side of the foyer and finds himself staring at a wooden staircase. Some of the steps are crooked and the handrail has missing posts. A young woman with frizzy hair appears at the end of the hallway that runs alongside it, led by the hand by a young boy. When she sees the Operator, her eyes fall to the blaster in his hand.

The scared woman kneels down and shields the young one with her body. "What do you want?" she yells, turning her neck so the Operator is still in her sight.

"Ta-taxes," the Operator says, his voice catching in his throat. He holsters his weapon. "I'm sent by the White Jackets—you haven't paid."

The woman becomes indignant at the mention of the White Jackets. She ushers her child into the adjacent room and stands up, brushing her shirt flat. "We haven't paid because there's nothing to pay! We're barely scraping by as it is."

"Look, lady, just give me what you can and be done with it."

"Or what?" the woman says, her hands on her hips, her blue eyes resolute.

The Operator wonders why he ever assumed tax collection would be as easy as showing up and reminding the residents they have to pay. "The White Jackets are always looking for new members," he says while leaning over and looking up the staircase. "They've found that raising them from childhood produces the most loyalty."

The color drains from the woman's face. "You can't," she says.

"Oh, I won't—I have nothing to do with recruitment, or training." He levels his eyes at her and adopts a serious tone. "Think of me more like the muscle."

The mother thinks for a moment then tells the Operator she'll be back. When she returns, she throws a small bag with a few plastic disks jangling around inside at the Operator.

He shakes it. "This it? Are they full?"

"Yes, and yes. Though one of the whites might be a partial," she says, furious. "I told you, we don't have much. We'll have to go hungry as it is."

"You can eat what's in that garden of yours," the Operator says, shaking the disks into his hand—a handful of white and two blues.

The mother makes a sucking sound with her teeth. "We can only eat what he gives us, which isn't much," she says.

The Operator looks at her. "He? Who's he?"

For the second time since he's been there, the woman looks terrified. "Forget I said anything."

"It's not some big secret—I already saw the garden. Just tell me who it is and where I can find them."

The woman closes her mouth and squeezes her lips together.

"Fine then. I'll find *him* eventually." He takes a blue chip from the collected group—it can hold up to one million credits, making it much more valuable than the white—and flicks it, sending it in a long arc that ends at her feet.

"For food," he says, nodding towards the door where the child disappeared. He leaves before she can make a sound.

On a whim, the Operator crosses the street and starts his search for residents on the far side of the street. He strikes out three times before finding an empty alley filled with bright food wrappers—the rest of the litter in the area has been an aged, dingy gray. There's a metal staircase leading to the second floor. He walks up, taking careful steps so he doesn't make a sound, and finds himself looking through an empty doorframe at a row of doors, fresh litter outside each. He walks down the hall, inspecting each door, wondering how he'll get money from so many residences—as soon as he leaves the first home, the person could alert all the others while he's in the second.

The only way onto the level, other than the external staircase at the end of the hall, is by a staircase in the center of the hall. The Operator, standing in front of it, fires three shots into the ceiling and yells, "Everyone out!" while debris falls onto his head.

Three doors open and three pairs of eyes peer at the unexpected guest in the hallway: two old men—one with a bushy gray beard and the other sporting a dark gray mustache—and a young woman. One of the old men slams his door shut and the other two follow suit.

"Okay," the Operator says with a forced laugh. He walks across the hall to the closest door that opened and kicks it down.

"What'd you do that for?" the bearded old man snarls.

The Operator doesn't respond. Instead, he proceeds to the adjacent door and kicks it down too, finding an abandoned room. Within minutes, every door in the hall hangs from its hinges and a storm of angry residents from seven apartments stare at him with eyes full of rage. Only a few of the residences were abandoned. A young man, urged on by an older woman at his back the Operator assumes is his mother, rushes the Operator until he's staring down the length of a barrel.

"Back up," the Operator says.

The dutiful son returns to his mother's side.

"Now that I've got your attention," the Operator says. "What do you know about the garden across the street?"

"You kicked down our doors for *that?*" says the old man with the beard who first slammed his door shut.

"I asked everyone to come out first. Nobody listened."

"The garden belongs to Eric Nieto. He showed up a few years ago and took over that block," the resigned old man says.

"Everyone over there reveres him like he's some sort of big shot," the mother of the older son says. "He gives them a few fruits and vegetables and all of a sudden he's king of the world."

"How do I find him?"

"Rumor has it that he has a hidden door in one of the lower-level spots. Don't know which one though. Probably all of them, if I had to guess," the second old man, the one with the mustache, says, emboldened by the revelations provided by the others.

"Does he sell food?"

"To those who can afford it," the son says, his voice heavy with sadness. "It isn't cheap."

Everyone hangs their head in shame.

"Okay, speaking of money—I'm also here from the White Jackets. Tax collection."

Everyone in front of the Operator stares at him like he murdered their firstborn. In a flash, he wonders how many he could take down before their numbers overtake him. Odds are they would never get within arm's reach of him.

"Why do we even need to pay taxes? We don't get anything down here, below the reclaimers," the old man with the mustache says.

"Protection."

"From who? You all are the only ones coming to bother us!"

"From Sigma thieves taking advantage of people on the border." Klepsydra's primary justification.

The grumbling begins, accompanied by eyes meeting eyes with quick nods in his direction.

"Look, I'll make a deal with you," the Operator says, holding both hands up, his blaster pointed to the ceiling. "Since it sounds like this Eric guy owes way more taxes than all of you combined, and you all gave me some information, hand over five blue credits between the lot of you and we'll call it even."

"You think we have that?" the mother yells. "Hell, I'd kill for that much!"

"You might have to," the Operator says, meeting her eyes.

Everyone turns to the two old men. "I'll hand it over, but you all owe me," says the old man with the mustache. He disappears into his room and emerges holding the disks in his hand. "Been saving for years," he grumbles.

"Oh quiet, you know we'll pay you back," the bearded old man says.

The Operator accepts the disks with a warning that they'd better not be partials. He looks at the two old men standing near each other and realizes they must be brothers. "Are you two related?" he asks.

"We all are," says the young woman, one of the first to open their door. The mustached old man shushes her.

"You have our money, you thief. Now go away," the bearded man says, stepping out of the path between the Operator and the external staircase.

The Operator holsters his blaster and leaves the family with their broken doors and lighter wallets, leaving in search of more taxpayers across the street.

Nobody on the block surrounding the garden knows where Eric Nieto lives—or so they say. They all pay the Operator what they can and clam up at the first mention of the garden growing right behind their homes. He walks through each place, keeping an eye out for secret doors or evidence of foot traffic that doesn't make sense given the home's layout and occupancy. None of them even have the garden in sight. As the afternoon settles in, he stands in the shadow of the barrier between Gamma and Sigma on the next block, on the back side of the building he first entered, without finding anything else out about Eric Nieto.

Tired of playing games and no longer caring about ruining the garden's protective covering, the Operator goes back around the building to the first home he entered, hell-bent on tearing down the barricade and plastic sheet blocking his access. Once inside, he can find how Eric gets inside himself.

Inside the abandoned property, he walks through the front room and down the hall. This time, before turning right into the kitchen, he looks into the room on the left—a former office, complete with wooden desk and a built-in bookshelf filled with decaying books. One book, propped up against the far side, catches the Operator's eye—it isn't decaying and looks like it's brand new. Confused, he approaches the bookshelf and reaches out for the book, tilting it back along the spine.

The book stays suspended mid-fall at a forty-five-degree angle. Then, the entire wall shifts back with a groan, exposing dark cement floors. The Operator pushes against the wall and it glides back

Inside, a small man with a round belly who looks like a mouse stares at the Operator with wide eyes before taking off at a full sprint.

CHAPTER SEVEN

THE OPERATOR WEAVES through the dozens of pots on the floor that host tender green shoots springing up from the soil. Most of the room's light comes from the fixtures positioned above the growing plants, none of them above his waist. The sole overhead light is in the kitchen where he caught the man by surprise, its flickering light hanging over an island counter illuminating accumulated gardening tools. His steps leave footprints in the thin layer of dirt as he follows the man through the attached hall. When the man turns off to his right, the Operator follows.

The room he enters has one other door that leads into the garden oasis. The Operator bursts between two sheets of plastic and meets a wave of humidity. Despite the calming smell of rich earth and greenery, he maintains his resolve as he turns left and walks through the shoulder-height plants. Leaves brush against his shoulders as he searches for the fugitive man with his blaster drawn, prepared for any act of retaliation. He calms his breathing, listening for footsteps.

A slice through plastic comes from the far right corner of the courtyard, followed by a quick ripping sound and the breaking of plates.

The Operator hurries to the noise's source and dives through, emerging into a small musty room the size of a large closet. Walking through a thick open door, and standing on pieces of broken ceramic, he sees the woman and child he first took taxes from. When he glares at her, the mother positions herself in front of the young boy.

"I didn't know!" she says, referring to the hidden door—the back of the door has numerous shelves that once held their serving ware.

"Where?" he says between breaths.

The mother points towards the front entrance.

The Operator runs through the residence and bursts through the front door. The target is on his left, his head turned around while running as fast as his legs can carry him.

With a sigh, the Operator starts after him. The man slows down and tries turning into a door on his left, finding it locked. He tries again at the next door without success. By now the Operator is close behind.

"Eric Nieto," the Operator says, his voice deeper than usual.

At the mention of his name, the mouse-faced man turns around. His cheeks are red, and his chest rises and falls in time with his rapid breathing.

"Are you coming to kill me?"

"Kill you?"

"You're from the upper levels, aren't you?"

The Operator holsters his blaster. "Why would someone from the upper levels be down here?"

"Hunting me down."

"I'm hunting you, but not to kill you. Tax collection."

Eric Nieto breathes a sigh of relief and bends over, resting his hands on his knees. He inspects the Operator with amusement. "The White Jackets sent an android on tax collection? Seems like overkill."

"You can tell?" the Operator says, stricken with a sudden case of self-consciousness.

"Course I can! Worked on androids for a decade before I had enough—couldn't stand working for Jirasek," he says between heavy breaths.

"Did you know about his plan for the city?"

"No idea—I was surprised as anyone when the ship showed up overhead. I only helped develop the exterior characteristics, and that was years ago at this point."

The Operator nods. "Well, hand over your taxes and I'll be out of your hair," he says, all business.

"Sure, I've got it back at home."

"If you have it, why didn't you just pay?"

"How would I get it to them? Send it on a rat? I'm not walking all the way across the district if I don't have to," he says, slapping his round stomach with a smile. He walks past the Operator and waves a hand. "Come on."

Back in Eric's apartment, the Operator takes a look around while the horticulturist roots around in a metal lunchbox taken from one of the island counter's cabinets. Besides the door that leads to the room attached to the courtyard, there's one other room that isn't ignored—a small bedroom, with a short stool sitting next to a dirty mattress. Extra pots and bags of dirt are at the foot of the bed, as if Eric dreams of plants and wants materials handy for when he wakes up and wants his imaginings brought into reality.

Eric hands the Operator ten blue disks when he walks back into the kitchen. "They're all full," he says.

"You know I'll be back if they're not."

"I know," Eric replies, smiling. He's downright pleasant without the fear of death looming over his head. "Now I've got to figure out what to do about the entrance on the back side of the greenhouse," he says, thinking out loud to himself.

"They really didn't know about it?"

"Nope. I've been keeping an eye out, and there hasn't been anything missing. I wouldn't have minded if they stole a bit—it's a kid, ya know?"

The Operator nods.

"I'll probably just seal it for good," Eric says, his voice trailing off. When the Operator starts walking out without saying a word, he asks if he's heading back to the White Jackets.

"No reason for me to stay," the Operator says.

"Good. The others don't need to pay taxes—they don't have much to begin with."

"I already got their payments. They said your prices are high."

Eric's mouth falls open. "They said that? It's a fair price," he says, hurt.

"Well, they said it isn't cheap."

"Everything is expensive to them," Eric says, looking off to the side. Inspired, he turns back to the Operator. "Why'd you take their money? They don't have anything in the first place! I chose to be down here—they never had an option."

"Orders. Collect taxes from everyone."

Eric reaches into the metal lunchbox and grabs more disks. "I'll pay."

"Just give it to them."

"I can't. Once they start taking from me it won't stop."

"Not my problem," the Operator says, leaving. Eric Nieto's last words ring out from behind him as he walks through the secret entrance: "You can't just take from people and not provide anything in return!"

The Operator walks out into the street and looks around, wondering if he missed collecting from any other residents, perhaps the ones not on the ground floor. He reaches into his pocket, feels the collected disks, and decides he has enough—if Klepsydra has any issues, she can come back herself. The realization that, in essence, he took money from Gamma's less-privileged residents as payment for Lucy's protection doesn't sit well with him, but he brushes away the pit in his stomach and starts walking back to the market.

A scream from behind stops him in his tracks. He turns around and sees two young men chasing a teenage girl away from the barrier between Gamma and Sigma. Another man jumps down from the barrier, landing in a squat with a devilish grin pasted on his face.

Invaders from Sigma. "Not my problem, not my problem," the Operator says to himself, over and over, as he takes steps away from the barrier, battling Eric's parting words for supremacy in his mind. The Operator stops and takes a deep breath.

Klepsydra did say the taxes were for protection.

With a groan, the Operator turns around and watches the youths disappear into an alley, chasing down further screams. He breaks into a jog, aware of the disks of credit rattling around in his pocket.

Turning into the alley, the Operator finds the teenage girl protected by the two old men and the son from the second-story apartments, all four of them surrounded by the three larger Sigma invaders. The old man with the mustache has a deep cut above his left eye, and his brother has blood spotting his beard. When they see the Operator, the bearded brother points to the three invaders from Sigma and tells him to, "Get them!" Blood fills the spaces between his teeth.

The three attackers turn and face the Operator. Each of them snarl, exposing rows of pointed teeth, the Sigma body modification of choice. They look at the blaster on the Operator's hip. The Operator follows their gaze then looks at them again before smiling and holding his fists in front of his face, planting his right leg behind him, adopting a fighting stance.

The first man from Sigma launches a furious flurry of low kicks that forces the Operator backwards. He realizes the man has no idea what he's doing and relies on pure aggression. When he decides the time is right, the Operator twists himself and lunges forward with a kick of his own aimed at the man's supporting back leg, shattering his knee while absorbing his final kick on the back side of his striking leg. The man screams and goes down in a heap.

Both remaining men attack him together next. It's clear they work together often, because each of their strikes are timed for when the other prepares for the next. The Operator deflects a few rounds of attacks from each man before he realizes the opening in their style—since each goes for a knockout blow, there's a considerable windup time before the strike launches. Spinning outside the punch of the man on his left, the Operator hits him with a quick left jab on his right cheek. The other man comes around his stumbling comrade's back and swings a wild right haymaker, which misses the Operator, who leans back.

The Operator focuses his quick strikes on the first man, working around in a way that keeps the recipient between himself and the second attacker. The strikes add up, and the Sigma man's face transforms into a bright red mask of tender flesh. The sharpened teeth cut the Operator's knuckles when he hits the man's mouth, but the pain helps him focus.

"Get him!" the first attacker snarls from the ground, his voice a mixture of anger and pain.

The second of the two attackers, his face still untouched, pushes his comrade into the Operator. When the pushed man stumbles and falls, the Operator launches a rib-cracking uppercut into his side. The move exposes the right side of his face and a savage left hook lands square on his jaw. Stars cloud his vision, and the world turns as he stumbles, his eyes searching for the proper orientation.

Inspired by the downed man's urging, the last attacker rushes. He unleashes a punch to the Operator's midsection that finds its mark, expelling all the air from the Operator's lungs. A powerful right-legged kick lands on the outside of the Operator's left thigh.

The sensation of falling doesn't stop until the Operator's back finds the adjacent building's wall. He crunches with his elbows in tight and absorbs the continuous blows. All of a sudden, he hears a guttural scream from nearby.

The son and the two old men take down the final attacker and kick his midsection while the Operator stands back up. Convinced the man from Sigma isn't getting up, and seeing that the Operator is around in case he does, two of them peel off and begin kicking the other two invaders.

They don't stop until the men are unconscious. Even then, while the teenage girl begs them to stop, their rage is so engrossing that they don't recognize her pleas. It takes the Operator pulling the men back before they return to the alley from riding their waves of anger.

All three Sigma men groan with their first breaths when they wake up to light slaps from the Operator on their cheeks. They stare at the Operator and the Gamma residents with impotent rage.

"Get out of here, if you know what's good for you," the Operator says.

Somehow, all three men stand up. The two with working legs support the man with a shattered knee, though their ruined torsos make accepting any extra weight difficult. One man coughs and spits blood. The Operator walks behind them through the haze while they hobble down the alley and approach the barrier between Sigma and Gamma.

"They pay for protection," the Operator says, pulling out his blaster and inspecting it. He fires a few rapid rounds at their feet—the two supporting Sigma men drop the third. He hits the ground with a thud and a scream.

"Next time, I'll just shoot you," he says.

The Sigma men stare at the barrier looming over them. Somehow, they climb up and over and out of the Operator's life.

The Operator holsters his gun and turns around. He walks right by the grateful family without stopping, acknowledging their praise with a single head nod. Across the alley, Eric smiles before disappearing into his dilapidated residence.

CHAPTER EIGHT

A FLOOD of people fleeing from Gamma's market meet the Operator when he returns. He forces his way against the flow, and more than once a person with their head turned around almost runs right into him; when they do, he cushions the blow by grabbing shoulders and moving them out of his path.

His thoughts go to Lucy. "What's going on?" he asks the bodies streaming past.

Nobody answers him.

When the initial crowd thins, he sees the old lady from the stall where he bought his broom shuffling towards him as fast as her arthritic legs can carry her, leaning on her cane every other step. A young woman he hasn't seen before tries helping her multiple times, but each time the old woman lowers her shoulder and slouches until the supporting grasp falls off of her, gesturing with her own hand for the young woman to go on without her.

As the Operator rushes forward to ask her what's going on, a space opens up in the crowd and he sees why everyone fled the market—a line of skinless androids on the far side of the bridge that bisects the market march towards him, burning everything in their path. Their skeletons are gleaming silver, and the left arm of each has a flamethrower attached just above the wrist. Behind them, between the market and the abandoned train station, a larger version of the searching sentinel hovers just above the ground, smooth metal gleaming in the flames.

The stall owner recognizes him and gestures him to her side. "You have to do something!" she says, knowing his history.

The Operator looks at the androids again. In addition to the flames, they all have blasters attached to their right arm, their hands free. "Not my fight," he says, leaning over and putting an arm around the old lady, ushering her forward.

"Don't touch me!" the old lady says, lurching forward another step. The young woman next to her meets the Operator's eyes and sighs with a shrug.

"We're looking for a fugitive," one of the androids announces, their words booming over the sound of the destruction. None of them look like they're speaking—the sound comes from an internal speaker that could be inside any of them. "Hand her over and we'll leave."

The Operator realizes the androids want Lucy and stands up straight. This might be his fight after all.

Before the androids realize there's someone in the crowd who isn't running away, the Operator crouches behind an ancient rusted car, against which an opportunistic vendor set up a stall selling stuffed animals and children's toys. Using it for protection reminds him of the shoot-out with Bacas, and he remembers the shots that the man buried in five of his joints. Returning to the present, the Operator counts the approaching force—twelve androids. They walk as a single unit, waiting while those on the ends tear through burning stalls, unaffected by the fire. He takes out his blaster and takes aim.

His first shot finds the center android's head. They stumble backwards and the other eleven all stop their forward progress and raise their right arms. When the shot android stands back up and rejoins the line with his right arm also raised to the horizon, they all take another step forward in unison.

The Operator looks at his blaster, surprised the android took the shot and remained unaffected. Nobody but Jirasek has technology so advanced. Without any other options, he shoots the same android again, this time shooting at the raised blaster on his right arm. It explodes in a fireball, taking off the android's arm and sending it down in a heap.

Eleven androids take aim at the Operator's hiding place and concentrate their fire on the rusted vehicle, continuing their march forward and burning the stalls that stand in their way with their other arms.

Movement in a second-level window catches his attention. He sees a white sleeve holding a blaster rifle, long black hair down to the person's shoulders. Surveying the other second-story windows on each side of the street, he discovers two rows of shooters, all aiming at the incoming androids. After a moment, they all fire in unison.

The torrent of shots against his cover disappears. He peeks over the edge of the vehicle and sees the androids on the ground, all of them intact, knocked over from the more powerful blaster rifle shots. Then, ahead of him to the left, a stream of people—some wearing White Jackets, some not—emerge from the stall that hosts the entrance to their hideout, running into the street. They all take aim with their blaster pistols.

When the androids stand back up, the shooters on the ground pepper them with shots from their blasters. The weaker firepower doesn't knock any of them down, but they do take multiple steps back before bracing themselves against the sustained fire.

One of the shooters on the ground wearing a white jacket, one of the women who was with Klepsydra when the Operator last saw her, stops shooting and looks at the second-story shooters. "What are you waiting for?" she yells.

The second volley of blaster rifle shots hit androids already braced for impact. The momentum transfers through their body and out through their back feet, digging into the ground and creating mounds of raised asphalt behind them.

Someone flies down from far overhead, landing behind the entrenched androids in a kneeling stance, their hands also helping absorb the impact. Gleaming gunmetal shines through the debris displaced by their arrival. The Operator assumes it's another android until they stand up. It's a woman, her jet-black hair tied back in a way that leaves two strands framing the standard Enforcer glasses on her face. The gunmetal surrounding her body sits off of her skin, attached by rings at the neck, elbow, and knee and ending in gloves and boots, leaving her tattoo-covered arms exposed. Beneath the exoskeleton she wears black tights and a black tank top, the unmarked skin on her chest and neck pale white.

Before any of the android attackers turn around, she grabs the one in the middle, one hand on their neck and one on the crown of their head, and rips them apart.

Four more dark-haired women with exoskeletons and dark glasses land behind four other androids, dismantling them before the androids know they have an enemy at their back. When one of the remaining untouched androids takes aim at a member of her team, the first arrival pulls a shotgun from a back holster and fires from her hip, leaving a large hole in the android's center. Three of the new arrivals also take out shotguns of their own and attack the androids—the fourth prefers tearing heads from bodies after dancing around the gunfire.

The Enforcers holster their weapons and turn their attention to the ship parked on the ground between the market and the train station. The tattooed leader takes turns looking at each member of her team, communicating in unspoken gestures. All of a sudden, the two Enforcers on the end run forward at full speed. After they take a few steps, the Enforcers on each side of the leader begin running with a slow start, and the tattooed leader starts running last.

The two Enforcers at the front of the pack turn in, cutting an angle towards each side of the blue-green ovoid ship. At the same instant, the next two launch themselves into the air towards the buildings on each side of the street. The moment their feet come into contact with the building, they launch themselves even higher into the air, at a point well above the ship. The leader leaps when her two comrades hit the building, a powerful jump made possible by the exoskeleton surrounding her body. Her trajectory is more straightforward, aimed at a point just above the top of the ship.

Time stands still for the Operator for a brief moment, a vision of choreographed perfection in the haze, complete with flames reflecting off gleaming various-colored metal. Humans transformed into projectiles, all taking different trajectories while seeking their shared target.

The ship executes a smooth turn and brings time back into full speed, rotating so the thinner portion of the hull runs the length of the street and rises from the ground. When the center of the ship is where the top was a moment before, the center Enforcer slams into it with her shoulder, knocking it back. The two Enforcers who started running first are just past the ship. They each take their shotguns from their back holster and, instead of taking aim, jam the barrels into the ship at an angle that points back to where they came from, piercing the metal hull with a loud crunch. They dig their heels into the ground and arrest the ship's backward momentum.

A war cry emerges from the two Enforcers that launched themselves from the building. They each have their shotguns out as well and descend on the unmoving ship with the barrel between their bent knees. They land on the ship and bury their shotgun barrels deep inside, their momentum knocking the ship out of the air.

The leader, in a kneeling position on the ground where she landed after first hitting the ship, lifts her head when the ship makes contact with the asphalt. "Now!" she yells.

Four shotguns erupt, the two on the sides angled back at her sending electronic parts outside each of her shoulders. The ship shudders. The leader approaches the ship, rips off part of the hull, and shoots her own shotgun into the exposed wires, leaving the ship lying still.

After the skirmish, the five-person team walks back to the eliminated androids and surveys the damage while half the market smolders behind them. The White Jackets all keep their blasters on the new arrivals—they couldn't care less about being a target.

"Yoshiko!" an enraged Klepsydra calls out from one of the second-story windows. The tattooed Enforcer turns her head in the direction of the sound while the rest of her team stands behind her at an angle, making a *v* with her at the point.

Klepsydra shows up on street level after a few moments, storming out from a building across the street from the stall with the entrance to the hideout. "What are you doing here?" she demands.

Yoshiko makes a show of putting the glasses on top of her head before looking around at the decimated androids and ruined portions of the market. "Helping you out, I'd say," she replies.

"We had it under control," Klepsydra says, her hands in fists.

"You call this 'under control'?" Yoshiko says with a laugh. A stall at the edge of the flames collapses.

"This is my territory," Klepsydra says through gritted teeth.

"Only because nobody bothers installing a new Enforcer." Yoshiko watches as ash floats through the air and lands on her thigh. Brushing it off, she says, "Don't get ahead of yourself."

Klepsydra's shoulders rise as she takes a massive breath. The Operator thinks she's preparing for a verbal assault, and he's surprised when she lets the air out without saying a word. "Back to my original question—what are you doing here? You've never cared about our problems before."

"Never had to. But now that Bacas went and got himself killed, there's nobody I can reach out to when I need something."

The Operator looks around at the mention of Bacas, wondering if Yoshiko has any idea that he's the one who made Bacas disappear.

"Well then, what do you need?" Klepsydra asks.

"Same reason they're here, I'm guessing," Yoshiko says, kicking one of the dismembered androids on the ground. "An android named Lucy. We sent another team down but they disappeared. You wouldn't happen to know anything about that, would you?"

The Operator feels time slow down. A flurry of thoughts race through his mind, each more disturbing than the last. He wonders if trusting Klepsydra was wrong, if she'll help the Enforcers so she can earn some credit with them, if Lucy's already tied up and ready for handing over, or worse, murdered, dead inside the theater.

Klepsydra puts her hands on her hips and glares at the Enforcer. The Operator holds his breath.

"Never heard of her. Or your missing team," Klepsydra says.

"No matter," Yoshiko says with a shrug. She lowers her chin and meets Klepsydra's stare. "Jirasek will send more," she says. "And I'm not sure if we'll be around to save your—" She looks around and gestures with her hand to the surrounding market. "Whatever this is."

"Let 'em. They won't find anything."

Yoshiko steps forward and juts her chin out while tilting her head. Her lips turn down into a confused frown. "If I find out you're hiding her—"

"Yes, I'm keeping her hidden when handing her over would've stopped this destruction. I don't know her; I'd give her to them, to you—doesn't matter to me. Don't be ridiculous." With that, Klepsydra turns around and waves her hand above her shoulder. "Be seeing you," she says.

Yoshiko stands tall before pointing into the sky. At the signal, Yoshiko and the rest of her team launch themselves at the nearby buildings, aided by the exoskeletons, all of them hitting the buildings at a point above the third-level reclaimers. They scramble up and disappear around the corner.

CHAPTER NINE

"I can't stand her," Klepsydra says while shaking her head when the Operator gets to her side.

"Thanks," he says.

"I didn't do it for you. Or Lucy. I'm not helping *her* under any circumstances. Let her find her own android if she's so smart!" she says, lifting her chin to the building Yoshiko disappeared around.

The Operator follows her and a group of her White Jacket cronies through the door she emerged from into the street, taking an unfamiliar series of corridors to the theater. There, they find Lucy sitting by herself in the first row of seats in front of the stage. The fugitive gets up when she hears the group approach.

"You're quite popular," Klepsydra says to her as she walks down the aisle.

Lucy looks confused.

"Another team of Enforcers came down looking for you," the Operator informs her.

"More? What do they want from me?"

"I was hoping you could tell us. It's not just them either—

Jirasek sent a team of androids. Destroyed half the market." Klepsydra climbs onto the stage and sits down at the head of the table. She levels a stern gaze at Lucy. "Why don't you just start at the beginning."

The Operator almost interjects on Lucy's behalf before she starts speaking. "I don't remember anything before waking up in the pool hall, with him and Miguel," an embarrassed Lucy says, pointing to the Operator.

"So you really have no idea why everyone's looking for you? The most powerful person in the city just sends his team to the surface for no reason?"

"I didn't say for no reason. I said I don't remember."

"How convenient," Klepsydra says, crossing her arms and leaning back in her chair.

"Who was that Enforcer in charge? You two seemed to know each other," the Operator says, changing the subject.

"*That Enforcer* is Yoshiko Apocalypse—head Enforcer in the city. The others are the rest of her squad."

"She's impressive," the Operator says.

"Tell me about it," one of Klepsydra's White Jacket cronies says in awe. "The way she just dropped down and—" She stops speaking when she notices Klepsydra's glare.

"What's impressive is that she's down here putting her nose in our business in the first place," Klepsydra says. "Jirasek has the city under siege and she's tearing apart androids on the surface—it makes no sense."

"Maybe she saw a chance for a fight," the Operator suggests.

"Or maybe our friend here has something to do with the ship hovering over the city," Klepsydra says while inspecting Lucy.

"Does she always wear the gear?" the Operator asks, again turning the conversation away from Lucy.

"Not always. Only when she and her team are expecting a

fight. I've never even seen the tech in action, just heard about it."

"Jirasek will think twice before putting boots on the ground again," the Operator says.

"Lucky for him he doesn't really have to. Those smaller ships of his are making quick work of everything flying in the city—there's nothing down here but us." Klepsydra looks at Lucy again. "Makes you wonder why he risked it looking for her."

Lucy is uncomfortable with Klepsydra's attention.

"It's been a long day," the Operator says after an uncomfortable silence.

"It has," Klepsydra agrees. "And we'll have to guard the market while they rebuild tomorrow. Why don't we all get some rest? Be ready to go first thing in the morning," she says, addressing those under her command. She doesn't stand up when everyone, including Lucy and the Operator, filters from the stage.

"Are you forgetting something?" Klepsydra adds. Everyone turns around and sees her staring at the Operator. The White Jacket's leader raises her eyebrows at him.

"Oh yeah," he says, returning to the table and taking the sack of disks from his pocket.

"You go on, I won't keep him long," she says to Lucy.

Klepsydra waits until the two of them are alone before dumping the disks on the table and counting her haul of credits. "Did you run into any trouble?"

"Three men from Sigma, had to take care of them." A troubling thought emerges from the depths of his stomach. Something he hadn't considered until that moment. "Wait. Did you know they were coming?"

Klepsydra takes her time stacking the chips into color-coordinated piles. "I knew there was a chance."

The Operator slams a fist onto the table. The disks scatter. "What if I wasn't there?"

"Well, you were," Klepsydra says, looking at the knocked-over piles. Her flexing jaw pulls at the bird wings on her neck tattoo.

"They can't defend themselves."

"And so I sent you."

Klepsydra leaves the pile of chips in front of her and places both hands on the table before turning her head and meeting the Operator's furious gaze. "Look, they've come over on a regular schedule and I guessed they would follow their routine. And you were there to teach them a lesson." She chuckles. "Think you did enough for them to think twice before coming over again?"

"One guy has a shattered knee, and all three were beaten to a pulp by the people living nearby."

"Oh good! So they're taking some responsibility for protecting themselves! That's what I like to hear."

"They'll get hurt if they try again by themselves!" the Operator yells.

"And they shouldn't have to, now that the boys from Sigma know what can happen!" Klepsydra raises her voice too, but there's a mocking tone hidden within.

The Operator realizes Klepsydra's conviction; she won't budge. He exhales, calming himself. "They don't have much," he says, gesturing towards the disks on the table.

"I see that," Klepsydra says, stacking the handful of white chips on top of the blues. "You get what you pay for."

The Operator stands tall, takes a deep breath, and walks away without another word.

"I'll see you in the morning. And make sure Lucy understands that she has to stay inside!" Klepsydra says to the Operator's back as he leaves the stage.

The next morning, Lucy is furious when she finds out about Klepsydra's decision. "Stay in here? Alone? I was alone the whole time you were gone!"

"You were?" the Operator says, leaning against the wall in her room. It was once a dressing room, with two large cabinets on each side of a cracked mirror.

"They said it was for my *protection*. Two White Jackets positioned themselves outside of this door—" She points to the lone entrance to her room. "And scurried away whenever I needed anything. They didn't outright say I was their prisoner, but I knew without being told."

"This is for your protection too," the Operator says. Klepsydra never told him the rationale for Lucy staying inside, but he can guess. "Both Jirasek and the Enforcers are looking for you, and Klepsydra told them she doesn't know where you are. You're at risk if you go into the market, and you put a target on her back too."

"But the market's destroyed because they were searching for *me*. The least I can do is help rebuild!"

"You can help by making sure the destruction wasn't pointless." The Operator stands up from his spot on the wall and readjusts his holster. "And that means not getting caught if they come back."

Lucy's disappointed eyes bore into him before she turns away in a huff.

"I'll come get you afterwards and we can figure out what to do next," he says, leaving her room. He meets the rest of the White Jackets in the theater during Klepsydra's speech.

"We can't count on Yoshiko coming back if more androids show up," she says. "Keep your eyes to the sky for any of Jirasek's transport ships—if one looks like it's coming below the reclaimers, fire your blaster into the sky. The rest of us will hear it." She then delegates different areas for her created teams, saying they can help those in the market as long as one of their group is on the lookout.

"What if there are android spies among the crowds?"

"Like they land far away and pretend they're human," another one says, looking at the Operator with wary eyes.

The Operator temporarily forgot about the attitude towards androids and wonders if recent events harmed the reputation of those with inorganic intelligence even further.

"Keep an eye out for those too. But I don't think that's Jirasek's style," Klepsydra says. "Any other questions?"

When none come, she offers one last piece of advice. "Remember, we're out there so the Gamma residents see who protects them—we can't have them clamoring for Yoshiko whenever something goes wrong."

The gang nods in agreement and files out of the theater, through the path back to the stall that serves as their main entrance, and out into the market. As the teams disperse, Klepsydra tells the Operator that he's with her. The area of the market untouched by fire doesn't have a single open establishment, the fabric flaps in front of shops hanging down and hiding the wares within from view. Besides the White Jackets marching off to their assigned areas, the intact portion of the market is abandoned.

On the far side of the market, the area burned by Jirasek's androids, scores of people work together sorting the massive amounts of goods left in various stages of ruin. Where each stall once stood, its former owner oversees the teams comprised of Gamma's residents—the stall owners who escaped the destruction unscathed and scores of customers—telling them which items are salvageable and which are garbage.

"They aren't worried someone will steal?" the Operator says.

"Look around," Klepsydra says. She continues before the

Operator has the chance for another word. "Everyone from the district is here—well, those from nearby at least. And now we're out here too. Do you think anyone in their right mind will bother stealing? They'd be ostracized."

The Operator wonders if social pressure has that much of an effect on people living in a daily struggle for survival. He's certain that those living on the edge between Gamma and Sigma wouldn't worry about being accepted if it meant they had a measure more comfort or security in their lives. But he's glad Klepsydra has faith in her community.

They walk by a spot near the middle of the market where a stall once stood. There's little left besides a few pieces of the metal bracing that comprised the stall's skeleton. Recalling the layout, the Operator remembers that the space once held a blanket salesman's operation—no surprise there's nothing left after a fire.

"Why are you bothering with Lucy?" Klepsydra asks, breaking the silence between them.

The Operator chokes on his initial answer—that she reminds him of a woman he left behind long ago—and says, "She needed help."

"But this is getting a bit much, isn't it? I mean, now that you know Jirasek's looking for her, why bother?"

"I knew Jirasek was looking for her before. There was a sentinel searching with a spotlight."

"And you thought to yourself, 'Why not take on the man who took over the city?'" She reaches over and taps his head. "Everything all right in there?"

The Operator jerks away. "Don't," he says.

"Fine," Klepsydra says, pulling her hand back. "And Yoshiko Apocalypse wants her too? This might be more than even you can handle."

"Thanks for the warning."

"Warning, and an explanation. She'll get caught if she stays here. All it takes is one wrong word to someone, a small confession—"

"You don't trust your own gang?"

"I trust them, but I also know the limits. They have loved ones, friends, relatives. One word to them, and another to the stall owners who just lost their entire livelihood, about how the one person the upper levels are looking for is holed up in the theater? There are too many people here who now want revenge. Not to mention the fact that she's an android—you know how that's going these days."

A woman glares at the Operator as he walks past. "I'm aware."

The Operator spots Miguel up ahead, helping one of the stalls recover their burnt belongings. Next to him is the woman the Operator bought the broom from, the one who always asks about the pool hall owner. They're kneeling shoulder to shoulder, her with a smile pasted on her face and him with a resigned look of focused concentration.

"The pool hall closed for the day?" the Operator says when he gets close to his friend.

"Still a bit of time left before we open," Miguel says without paying attention as he turns around. When he realizes that the speaking man is the Operator, he stands up and gives his friend a hug, whispering, "She won't leave me alone," when his mouth is next to the Operator's ear.

The Operator laughs and pushes Miguel away. "Were you here for this?" Miguel asks. When the Operator nods, he proclaims he's not surprised. "What happened?"

Klepsydra, who kept walking and now stands a few steps ahead, clears her throat. "I'll tell you later," the Operator tells his friend. He looks past Miguel at the kneeling woman enamored with him and waves. She waves back.

"I'll leave you two alone," the Operator says.

Miguel frowns and drops to his knees.

Klepsydra and the Operator take a few steps in tandem before she stops and turns in his direction. "Why don't we hand her over? It's only a matter of time before they come back—we don't need to be involved in these upper-level politics."

The Operator's eyes open wide. When he twists and looks back at the theater, Klepsydra puts an arm on his shoulder.

"She's safe. For now. But like I said, it's only a matter of time before someone finds out she's here. We should get ahead of the issue."

The Operator shakes his head no. "Your gang's loose lips aren't my problem."

"I'm just being realistic! The people chasing her, they're too powerful. You don't need to make their problems your own. Just go back to the pool hall with Miguel and leave the rest to me."

The Operator tilts his head and turns up his lip in disgust. Without another word, he walks back through Gamma's market towards the theater, leaving Klepsydra alone behind him.

CHAPTER TEN

The Operator storms past the two White Jackets guarding Lucy's room. She's sitting on a chair, leaning back with her head dangling over the headrest, staring at the ceiling. The sound of the slamming door startles her upright.

"We're leaving," the Operator tells her.

Lucy stands up in a rush. "Where are we going?" she asks.

"Away from here. Grab your things."

She looks at the Operator with confused bemusement. "I don't have anything," she says.

"Right. Then let's go."

The two guards stand shoulder to shoulder in front of the door after overhearing the escape plan. "She can't leave," one of them says.

The Operator, standing between the guards and Lucy, broadens his stance. His hand hovers over his blaster. "Are you sure you want to do this?"

The White Jackets look at each other. After a wordless exchange, they each take out their own blasters and point them at the Operator. "Told you: she can't leave."

Lucy steps around the Operator and puts a hand over his

blaster's barrel. "We don't need to do all this," she says, both of them holding the weapon at his side. She tries catching the Operator's gaze with her own, but he won't terminate the stare-down. Continuing forward, she steps in front of the White Jackets. They move enough so they can continue aiming at the Operator from over her shoulders.

"Why don't we wait until Klepsydra gets back. We're leaving, and we'll be out of your hair soon. She shouldn't have a problem with that. Isn't that right?" she says, turning around to the Operator for confirmation.

The Operator nods, his face otherwise expressionless.

"See? There's no reason for all of this." Lucy reaches her right hand out and forces one of the blasters down. When it's pointing towards the floor, she rests her left hand on the barrel of the second man's blaster. Before she can force it down, the man jerks away, pulling on his blaster.

It doesn't budge.

In a blur of movement, Lucy pulls the second man's blaster up so it's pointing to the ceiling while holding the first man's blaster still. Two shots erupt from the White Jackets, one finding the ceiling and the other the floor.

Behind Lucy, the Operator dives to the right while pulling his own blaster from its holster. By the time he gets into a kneeling position with his blaster aimed at the door, Lucy has both blasters in her hand.

The White Jackets stumble forward into the room, carried by their momentum from holding on to their weapons for too long. They regain their balance and stand up, ready for a fight, never seeing the Operator kneeling off to the side.

With a smile on her face, Lucy drops both blasters onto the ground. The two White Jackets rush her. Lucy dispatches both with two quick jabs while sidestepping away from their advance, leaving the pair with broken noses.

It all happens before the Operator gets back to his feet. Lucy looks at him and points to the door with a tilt of her head. As they leave, the two White Jackets scramble for their surrendered blasters.

"This way," the Operator says, holstering his weapon and taking off at a sprint. Lucy stays right behind him, matching his pace step for step. They turn a corner as two shots from the White Jacket guards hit the wall behind them. Emerging into the theater, they jump down from the stage and begin running through the rows of seats towards the entrance they came through when they first arrived from Gamma's market.

Klepsydra appears at the door in front of them. She takes a few steps into the theater before stepping to the side, giving the retreating pair plenty of space. She doesn't say a word as they pass, and as the Operator leads Lucy out of the theater he hears her call out to the pursuing White Jackets: "Let them go."

The Operator leads Lucy to the staircase that descends into the midline. They take the stairs two at a time and burst into the darkness of the abandoned train tunnel.

"Don't need to run anymore," the Operator says, slowing down to a walk. He notices he's breathing harder than her.

"What are the midliners going to do if they find out we're back down here?" Lucy asks.

"Usryd lives on the other side of the train station," the Operator says, gesturing behind them. He puts his hand down when he realizes Lucy can't see him in the dark. "And we never saw any on this side the last time I was here."

They walk in silence, both recovering from their hurried escape.

Something shuffles up ahead. "What was that?" Lucy whispers.

They pause, listening. "When was the last time you were down here?" Lucy asks, again in a whisper.

"This isn't the first time I've had to leave the White Jackets behind."

"That doesn't answer my questions. How long has it been?"

"Not long enough." He resumes walking along the train tracks with Lucy at his side.

The patter of rapid footsteps comes from the walls on both sides. Then, something hard strikes the Operator on the left arm. He hears a dull thud as a projectile strikes Lucy on his right.

"Stop!" the Operator yells.

"Get out!" a low voice responds.

"I'm friends with Usryd," he says, his arms protecting his head.

The incoming projectiles don't stop. Instead, they increase in frequency.

"Go back where you came from!" says a raspy voice, different from the first.

The Operator reaches out and ushers Lucy ahead of him with a hand on her back before breaking out into a run. "Come on!" he urges.

Lucy doesn't need telling twice. Together, they run through the darkness, stumbling on the tracks and occasional debris in their path. The midliners give chase, staying close to the walls on the far sides of the support pillars that run along the tracks. Since they move on all fours, their strikes against the ground aren't as loud as the Operator's and Lucy's heavy footfalls. It also makes determining the number of pursuers impossible.

The midliners can't keep up with the Operator's and Lucy's long strides. Despite losing ground, they keep up the chase as they fall farther behind. The Operator turns around, looking for hints of movement, or the whites of eyes and teeth. His foot catches and he stumbles, falling to the ground. He tries getting back up and finds his heavy boot stuck. No matter how hard he pulls, his foot doesn't budge.

Lucy doesn't realize. She's still running, and the Operator hears both Lucy's footsteps getting farther away and the soft patter of quadruped runners approaching him from behind.

The Operator tries moving whatever it is that holds his boot in place. It doesn't work. The midliners get closer, their speed increasing with the fresh hope of catching the intruder.

He starts untying his boot, his fingers clawing at the tight knot. It's loose when the first midliner slams into him, twisting his body and putting immense pressure on his knee. He throws the midliner off of him and finishes untying the knot. His fingers are underneath the top laces, loosening them, when two more midliners reach him and throw their full weight on top of him.

Hoping he has enough slack in his laces, he pulls his foot—it moves within the boot but doesn't come free. He pushes the midliners away from him while they scratch and claw at his torso, their fingers searching for his face. With a mighty shove, he pushes them to each side and sits up, reaching for his shoelaces. All three attackers pull on his shoulders from behind while he struggles forward. They stay in a frozen stalemate until another midliner joins the fray, launching themself at the Operator from the front and forcing him back down with a thud.

His hands protect his face while jagged, uncut fingernails scratch at the fabric covering his forearms, searching for his eyes. Calloused hands grab onto his, prying them apart.

A kick from Lucy, who turned back when she realized the Operator was no longer behind her, sends a midliner flying through the air. They land with a whimper. A second strike finds its mark and something cracks within a midliner's body before it tumbles away. The third midliner finds themself grabbed by the shoulders and slammed into the ground. The fourth midliner lunges at Lucy with a yell. She brings a knee up straight in front of her and sends the midliner back through the air; they land on the Operator and take the wind from his lungs before continuing to the ground by his side.

While Lucy deals with the midliners, the Operator sits up and removes his foot from the boot. Without his foot stuck inside, he bends his boot and pries it free. A midliner jumps onto his back, sending him sprawling. They claw their way up to his face. He grabs the midliner by the neck with one hand and punches their face with the other, knocking them out. He searches in the dark for his boot.

"What are you waiting for?" Lucy yells out over the grunts and groans of the midliners.

"My boot," the Operator says. On his knees, he feels around in the dark until he finds it. Then, he puts it on his foot and ties a quick knot.

Lucy helps him back to his feet. All of the midliners either lie in an unconscious heap or are too broken for a continued assault. The pair take off at a measured jog, careful where they step.

"Why'd you stop?"

"My foot got stuck."

"Have to be careful in the dark," Lucy says. She can't see the Operator flex his jaw.

They emerge from the train station in Sigma in the middle of the day. The ship overhead still blocks the sun, but the residents in Sigma see a different part of the craft from their position in the city: the massive open port. Jirasek's smaller sentinels stream through the opening in the ship on their way to the city below for their constant patrols. Because of the sun's disappearance, the functional neon billboards on the skyscrapers shine bright against the persistent darkness, illuminating the streets in the haze below the reclaimers. Some of the billboards are black

—companies who gave up advertising while Jirasek maintains control of the city.

"Wait a second," the Operator says, kneeling down. He reties his boot to his preferred tightness and stands back up.

Lucy smiles at a young boy holding on to the hand of what could be his grandmother. The elder woman puts her arm around the child and holds him close, hurrying away while giving Lucy a skeptical glare.

The Operator taps Lucy's arm with the back of his hand. "Don't open your mouth," he says.

"Why not?" Lucy says, indignant. "He was cute."

"You don't have teeth."

"Yes I do," Lucy says, pulling her lips back.

The Operator makes a show of closing his own pursed lips. "You don't have *pointed* teeth."

"Oh, right," Lucy says. Her face relaxes as she closes her mouth.

"They won't know we're from Gamma because we don't have blue eyes," the Operator explains.

"Right. So I can look wherever I want."

"More or less," the Operator says with a nod.

The pair strike off in the direction of Regulo Pavlova's night-club, Chance. There are more people out in Sigma than the Operator's ever seen before, and he wonders if it has anything to do with Jirasek's ship looming overhead. The presence of children, a rare sight outside of the city's dedicated educational facilities, inspires a guess that families took back their offspring when disaster became a real possibility. Groups of people of all ages congregate on street corners, crowded around opportunistic street food vendors.

A loud screech erupts from overhead, the sound of microphone feedback. Then, every visible billboard—including the ones that were dark a moment before—lights up with a handsome, middle-aged face. His black collar is visible beneath a week-old beard that frames a strong jaw.

"For those who don't know who I am," the projected face begins, holding the attention of everyone on the ground. The audio and video are out of synch.

"My name is Felipe Jirasek. I'm coming directly to you, the citizens, for help."

An image of Lucy appears on the screen.

"I'm looking for this woman. Anyone who brings her to me or provides information about her whereabouts will find themselves and their families elevated to at least the seventy-fifth level. You know what that means—you'll be above the tropical paradise on the seventy-fourth, and can go there whenever you want."

The image of Lucy disappears, replaced by Jirasek once more.

"Paint an X with a circle around it as big as you can, wherever you are, and one of my ships will come investigate." He pauses for dramatic effect. "Best of luck to the citizens of the best city on the planet!"

CHAPTER ELEVEN

A HUM of conversation erupts as the billboards return to their previous state. First, the Sigma residents look at the friends and family by their side, discussing the new development. When it hits them that they have the opportunity for a life in the upper levels, dozens of levels higher than any of them ever dared dream, they look around, inspecting the faces in their immediate vicinity.

The Operator pulls Lucy into an alley, hoping nobody saw them. They crouch behind a dumpster.

"Do you think—" Lucy whispers.

"Hope not."

Nearby rats take notice of the visitors and approach them with noses wiggling in the air. They scatter when the Operator makes a wide sweep with his boot.

"I think she went down here, Mom," a child's voice says from the end of the alley. The Operator leans forward and peeks out, hoping that somehow the child isn't referring to their hiding place.

He is. It's the young boy Lucy smiled at when they first got into Sigma. His hand isn't in his mother's any longer; instead, he's pointing a small finger at the Operator.

"There!" the child says, pleased with himself.

The aged mother appears around the corner of the building and scoops up her child when she sees the Operator peering at them from behind the dumpster. She turns and yells, "They're over here!"

Three young men come running around the corner. "I just saw the guy she was with," the mother says as they run past.

The Operator joins Lucy in leaning back against the wall. "They've found us," he informs her. The men's footsteps slow to a walk.

"What are we going to do?" Lucy says.

The Operator leans to the side so he can withdraw his blaster.

"You can't shoot everyone!" Lucy hisses.

The Operator looks at Lucy with raised eyebrows, as if her statement were a dare. Then, he sighs. "Come on," he says, putting his hand on her knee and using it for help while he stands up.

"Easy, gentlemen," the Operator says as he emerges from behind the dumpster, aiming the blaster at the three approaching men. They flash their pointed teeth in wicked smiles. More curious people turn the corner at the end of the alley, pausing when they see the blaster held in their direction. Some back away, some move to each side of the confined space, and the bravest in the group stalk forward, ready for action. The Operator extends a hand and helps Lucy stand up.

Eyes widen when they spot the woman who makes the elevation of them and their family possible.

One of the three men closest to the Operator spits on the ground, then says, "Can't shoot all of us." He takes a rapid step forward, feinting a quick approach, and the Operator fires his blaster at the ground in front of his feet.

"Why don't you come find out?" the Operator says.

Lucy, standing behind the Operator, taps his back. The Operator turns his head to the right and leans back, just enough so he can see both her and the approaching men through his peripherals. Lucy jerks her head to the side, signaling towards the rest of the alley behind them.

The man who feinted his approach lunges forward, yelling out to the other men as he does. "Come on!" The Operator shoots him in the leg and he falls to the ground. The other two men pull up short.

Seizing the moment, the Operator turns and runs, making sure Lucy stays ahead of him. Behind them, dozens of men with pointed teeth start sprinting. The alley ends at a narrow street. Lucy starts turning left before seeing more men approach from that direction and deciding otherwise. The Operator helps her change direction with a tug on her arm.

They turn left onto a broader road at the end of the narrow street. The few people in the area are minding their own business—walking on the sidewalks next to the adjacent buildings or talking with friends—but the two people running for their lives grab their attention. When they recognize Lucy, they join in on the chase at the front of the pack.

The Operator turns and fires a handful of shots just over the heads of the closest pursuers, missing them on purpose. The Sigma residents in front, when they see the blaster's barrel aimed in their general direction, cover their heads with their arms and duck out of the way. The trailing pursuers stumble into them. The created mass of writhing bodies scramble forward, some crawling, all urged on by the potential for escaping life on the surface.

"Right!" the Operator says at the end of the next block.

Lucy, still ahead of him, turns onto another broad street. Nobody sits outside the dilapidated storefronts. Aged pieces of plywood cover every window, and empty spaces above doors are the lone remaining evidence of long-gone signs. They approach a rusted garage door on their right that extends through the second story. Bright orange graffiti covers it at ground level, and a flash of bright metal near the ground catches the Operator's eye. It's a brand-new lock, holding the garage door down by fastening it to a rusted brown metal loop buried in the cement.

The Operator shoots the lock and it transforms into a mass of twisted metal. "In here," he calls out to Lucy while pulling the mangled lock from the loop. She turns and meets the Operator at the garage door. They pull it up together. The Operator holds on to it as it raises, making sure it doesn't rise above head height. After the two of them scurry inside, the Operator pulls it down, closing it with minimal sound.

Together, they hold the garage door down using the weight of their bodies while listening for any approaching pursuers. Thunderous footsteps rush by outside the garage door, accompanied by people yelling, "Where did they go?" and, "Does anyone see them?"

The footsteps die down and the Operator feels himself relax. Lucy nudges him with her elbow. "Look," she says. He turns around.

The garage looks like it belongs on another level—at least the fortieth, if the Operator guessed without knowing. Illuminated by dim fluorescent lights, it extends far into the building, maybe even clear through to the next block. Rows and rows of hovercrafts sit in two lines, everything from sleek cruisers to industrial transporters. The pristine examples closest to him look ready for sale, while the ones near the back are in various stages of repair. The walls are a dark gray and lined with professional shelving, tools, and equipment he has never seen before. A pair of hydraulic lifts in the back support two vehicle shells.

Lucy stands up, leaving the Operator holding the garage door down alone. She steps forward in awe. "Who do you think this all belongs to?" she says, ignoring the volume of her voice.

The Operator lets go of his hold on the garage door and has one knee off the ground when voices outside pull his attention. He hears a faraway man giving orders through the metal door. "They're probably hiding in one of these places!" He imagines a finger pointing to the establishments on the block. "Let's find 'em!"

"They'll be here soon," the Operator says. He releases the garage door and runs between the rows of vehicles on the way to the back.

"Whoever owns all these won't be happy when they find out people are storming their garage," Lucy says. "Maybe they'll take care of the crowd for us."

"If they get here in time."

"We're here now," a husky voice says from the back of the garage. The voice belongs to a stocky man with a thick neck holding a blaster pistol in his hand. A thin man with a long, pointed face emerges behind him with a blaster rifle, the stock already resting against his shoulder.

The Dominguez brothers, car thieves who run the local street races.

"Do you know who we are? What the hell were you thinking coming—" The heavier man stops speaking when he recognizes the Operator. Then, his jaw drops when he sees Lucy.

"You!" the pointed-face man snarls while looking at the Operator. His brother nudges him in the ribs and juts his chin forward in Lucy's direction.

The thinner brother's eyes widen. "Does he want her dead or alive?" he asks.

"I don't know."

"Then we can't shoot to kill."

"Not her. But we can kill him."

"Agreed. Pavlova can't say anything about how we run our garage!"

"It's ours, after all."

By the time the two brothers finish hyping themselves up, the Operator and Lucy are inside a lustrous dark red hovercraft. It doesn't have a roof—clear evidence that it came from higher up, where the reclaimers purify the air. The keys are in the ignition, and it roars to life as soon as they sit down, emitting a smooth purr. Minimal interior lights shine a matching dark red on the black screen that comprises the entire dashboard.

The stocky brother aims his blaster pistol at the vehicle. Before he can shoot, his brother reaches out and pushes the blaster to the side. "Are you crazy?" he says. "She's worth more than the rest of the garage combined!"

After a slow, deliberate ascent, the sophisticated vehicle waits for the next command. The Operator feels the immense power under the hood—it's a quiet confidence inspired by the absolute knowledge of superior quality. He urges the vehicle forward with a smile, gliding over the other vehicles in the garage.

The Dominguez brothers run forward, pass the hovercrafts needing repairs, and jump into two vehicles close to the missing space left by the Operator. The garage door opens before they can take off, pulling the Operator's attention back to the street outside. A lone man looks at the Operator and Lucy in the high-performance vehicle. As he watches, the two hovercrafts piloted by the Dominguez brothers rise up. One gets behind the other along the center of the garage on their way out.

"In here," the ground pursuer yells. The Sigma residents emerge from all sides, joining the man who discovered the Operator's whereabouts at the entrance. After a brief pause, they storm inside in a singular mass.

The Operator's hovercraft is high enough off the ground that they can't touch him. He pushes the craft forward, increasing his speed over their heads. Some of the crowd jump onto nearby vehicles, using them as added height before launching themselves at the sleek dark red one flying by, but the smooth exterior offers no handholds. Each man claws at the glossy metal before falling back to the garage floor with a thud.

"Stay behind and guard the cars!" the pointed-face brother yells while turned around in the seat of his loud, dark blue hovercraft with sharp, aggressive lines. With a look of disappointment, the second brother turns his attention to the invading crowd while pulling out his blaster. "I swear I'll start taking heads!" he yells, opening the door of his vehicle and jumping onto the garage floor as the hovercraft descends.

The first brother returns his attention to the Operator and Lucy, urging his hovercraft forward with a growl.

Once the Operator and Lucy leave the confines of the garage, the Operator banks a sharp left, then a second, going back the way they came. Their hovercraft's superior handling and speed make creating distance between the chasing Dominguez brother and themselves simple: don't crash and stay moving. The Operator, guessing the beast the Dominguez brother drives can't handle sharp curves the same way his chosen vehicle can, turns into the narrow street he ran through earlier with Lucy, then into the alley where the child first alerted the residents about their hiding place. By the time he emerges onto the street they arrived on after leaving the midline, the Dominguez brother is gone, out of sight and without a sound.

Knowing that traveling by foot in Sigma is no longer an option, the Operator continues flying the hovercraft on the way to Pavlova's nightclub. He flies higher than normal, just below the reclaimers, so the Sigma residents on the surface don't see Lucy. When she tries leaning over the side of the door and looking at the street below, the Operator grabs her arm, telling her to "get back in here."

As they cross over an intersection halfway to their destination, the distant roar of an engine to their right demands their attention. In the distance, closer to the ground, is the Dominguez brother in his blue hovercraft, picking up both speed and altitude as he approaches their position.

The Operator pushes the hovercraft forward. The increase in speed pins him and Lucy against their seats. "Hold on," he says.

A loud explosion, followed by the screech of metal on asphalt, makes both the Operator and Lucy turn around. The blue hovercraft is on the ground far below, the wreckage still traveling forward—the pursuing Dominguez brother is motionless on the asphalt farther behind.

There's movement up in the sky. It's a blue-green ovoid, one of Jirasek's smaller sentinels, racing forward to their position.

"We flew too high!" Lucy says.

The Operator doesn't respond. He knows it, and feels guilty for forgetting about the risk.

Jirasek's ship focuses its spotlight on the dark red hovercraft and fires a flurry of shots as the Operator banks his vehicle to the left. One of the shots finds its mark, hitting the back end and sending them spinning. Out of control, the hovercraft slams into a nearby building before plunging to the asphalt below.

CHAPTER TWELVE

THE OPERATOR PULLS on the steering wheel, forcing the front of the hovercraft up as they plummet to the surface. Hitting the ground slams both the Operator and Lucy forward in their seats, the straps cutting into their torsos but holding them in place. Their momentum carries them forward, sending them crashing through the glass wall of a building. The skidding hovercraft turns on the ground but doesn't flip; the driver's side becomes the leading edge. Still conscious, the Operator spots the upcoming wall and leans towards the middle of the hovercraft. When the impact stops their motion, a portion of the wall sticks halfway into the Operator's seat, destroying half of the windshield and constricting his legs.

Jirasek's ship's bright spotlight through the hole in the building illuminates the wreckage. Smoke issues from beneath the hovercraft's engine. Dust and debris float back to earth. Lucy's head dangles forward while the seatbelt holds her upright.

"Wake up," the Operator says while coughing, reaching over and pushing on her shoulder.

There's no response.

The Operator reaches down and unlocks his seat belt. Then, he pushes Lucy's head back to the headrest with his left hand while reaching down and unlocking hers with his right. He puts both hands on the center console and pries his legs from the narrow space left for them, bringing his knees up onto the modicum of room left on his seat. Making it work requires an awkward contortion of his body, his hips turned along the hovercraft's length and his shoulders perpendicular, facing the passenger seat.

Lucy leans away from him when he lets go of her head. Her shoulder makes contact with the passenger door before she falls forward, her head hitting the dashboard with a thud.

Illuminated by the spotlight, the Operator climbs over Lucy and collapses onto the ground. An exposed piece of steel slashes his side, cutting through his shirt and the skin on his ribs. Still on his back, he looks at the pointed metal and releases a sigh of relief that he didn't land on it. He touches the gash then looks at the blood on his hand before wiping it clean on his pants.

The Operator gets to his knees then uses the hovercraft for support as he stands up. He can't hear a thing; his ears are still ringing from the sounds of the crash. Lucy's face still rests on the dashboard. He leans in and turns her body so he can grab her from beneath the shoulders. Then, cognizant of the sharp piece of metal on the ground, he pulls her from the smoking hovercraft. Her weight carries him forward when her legs clear the cabin. The two of them hit the edge of the hovercraft, him on top of her and the top of the hovercraft door digging into her lower back.

After pulling himself away, the Operator taps Lucy's face. "Lucy," he says, fearing the worst. Three more taps. "We've got to get out of here."

The Operator turns and looks at the spotlight, wondering

how long before reinforcements arrive. He grabs Lucy's shoulders and shakes. "Come on," he says.

Her head moves in all directions without any indication of control.

"Okay. Okay," the Operator says. He takes a few deep breaths before leaning forward and slinging Lucy over his shoulder. She's heavier than he remembers. Standing up with her makes the fresh cut on his side erupt in pain, the added pressure from braced muscles pulling on the edges of the wound. He takes a few uncertain steps on the shifting ground beneath him, torn up by the sliding hovercraft, before finding a solid area outside the path of destruction. Wires hang down from the ceiling from where walls stood moments before. Not knowing if the level has electricity, he avoids them while he walks towards the open door leading deeper into the building.

The march through the attached hallway is slow and laborious. His leg muscles ache, and his side sends searing pain through his torso every time his right foot strikes the ground. Reminding himself he's an android doesn't diminish the sensations, even though he knows everything he senses are simple electrical signals. Light filtering in from outside through barred windows seems dim compared to the brightness of the spotlight on Jirasek's ship. The doors he walks past are far apart, and each one opens up into a large space. Some are empty, some hold ancient cardboard boxes, and one filled with mannequins startles him until he realizes none of the human shapes move at all.

He drops Lucy in a heap in a nook created by the bottom of the stairs at the end of the hallway running behind the abandoned shops. Checking behind him, he sees the spotlight still shining through the door that leads to the crashed hovercraft.

"I'll be right back," he tells an unconscious Lucy, pulling out his blaster. He walks forward with long, quick strides, faster now that he doesn't have an android slung over his shoulder.

When he gets to the door, he puts his back against the wall and peeks into the wrecked room.

The ship that shot him down hasn't moved. He has a hard time believing he walked out of the hovercraft buried in the far wall even though it just happened. The wires hanging down sizzle and crack, the sparks lost in the spotlight. He aims at Jirasek's ship and fires.

The shot lands with a loud ding but the spotlight doesn't falter. He then fires a slew of shots and nothing happens. Jirasek's androids could arrive at any moment, marching past their alley and through the broken wall. Smoke rising from the wrecked hovercraft catches the Operator's eye. He aims his blaster at the vehicle and fires, hitting its front with a series of rapid shots. A tangle of internal wiring through the created hole emits sparks, a displaced hose hisses, and fluid from higher in the hovercraft guts leaks down on the carnage. The Operator fires a handful of shots again, stopping when he sees a flame. He waits for a second, making sure the fire doesn't die. It grows as he watches.

Knowing he has limited time available, the Operator turns and runs down the back hallway, passing the former retail spaces for a third time. He's almost to Lucy when the hovercraft explodes. The blast knocks him forward. Sprawled out on the ground with his head at Lucy's feet, he scrambles up as the pressure wave washes over them, covering her body with his.

The building emits a groan after the initial blast. The Operator lifts his head, listening. All of a sudden, there's a loud crash as the room where the hovercraft exploded collapses. A portion of the hallway soon follows while the Operator braces his head against Lucy again. There's a moment's pause each time the destruction meets a door, and it gets longer as the distance from the blown-up hovercraft increases. There's a long pause when the Operator lifts his head again and surveys the damage.

There's a single door remaining on his left—the rest of the hallway is gone. He pushes against the ground, away from Lucy. A rumble passes through the building and the final portion of the hallway collapses, leaving just the bottom set of stairs and the space where he hides with Lucy intact but covered in dust.

The Operator scrambles off of Lucy before the fickle building can collapse even further. She turns her head with her eyes still closed.

"Lucy!" the Operator says, putting his hand behind her head. "Come on, it's not safe."

Lucy exhales with a groan. The Operator places his other hand over her forehead, opening an eyelid with his dust-covered thumb. He wipes his hand before repeating the action on her other eye.

"Get up," the Operator says while holding her eye open.

Lucy's open eyeball snaps onto the Operator's face a moment before her other eye opens. She brings her knees up between them and extends her legs, sending the Operator flying through the air. His back slams onto the wall behind them and he slides down until his bent legs stop his downward motion.

"Good, you're up," the Operator says.

"Yes, I'm up," Lucy snaps. Every muscle in her face slackens. "I remember."

"Remember some other time," the Operator says, pulling Lucy up by the arm. "How do you feel?"

Lucy looks down at her legs, torso, and arms. Then, her eyes roll in the back of her head. "Everything seems all right," she says when her eyes refocus on the Operator.

"Let's go."

Lucy looks past the Operator at the rubble behind him. "What happened?"

"I'll explain later." He runs up the stairs and finds a window on the first floor. He opens it and looks out. Pulling his head back in, he says, "Jump."

Lucy takes a look at the open asphalt below, climbs through the window, and drops down, landing in a crouch. The Operator follows, falling after his feet strike the ground, his balance thrown off from the crash, wound, and explosion. He stands up and brushes himself off. "Keep moving," he says.

The Operator kicks down a door across the street and the pair rush into the building. They put as much distance as they can between themselves and the crash site, passing rat colonies, abandoned spaces, and families with playing children. The Operator keeps looking behind them as they run, worried that someone they pass will recognize Lucy and give chase. Eluding Jirasek's androids, the Sigma residents, and the faraway Yoshiko Apocalypse makes him suspicious of everyone and everything.

After a long time spent running, they end up in the burned-out building the Operator passed through when he was sent to Sigma on an assassination mission by Bacas. Despite the charred-out interior, the vast upper levels are safe from collapse because of an intricate web of supports attached between the building and its neighbors.

"We can rest here," the Operator says. He feels the wound on his side. The edges are hard scabs but the center hasn't healed at all because of the continuous exertion since he got injured.

Lucy takes a seat on the blackened staircase, her breathing regular and muscles relaxed—there's no indication of their time spent running. "I remember," she says for the second time.

"Remember the crash?" the Operator says. He winces when he pokes the injury on his ribs again.

"No. I remember where I came from."

The Operator looks at Lucy without moving his head.

Then, he wipes his hands on his pants and rushes over to the staircase, leaning against the wall. "Where?"

Lucy stares straight ahead. "I was sent to take down Jirasek's ship."

"No wonder they want you dead," the Operator says, his voice trailing off. He refocuses on Lucy. "By yourself?"

"I was one of a squadron of five. The leader pushed me out of our ship as the missile came in. The last thing I remember is falling through the sky."

"And then the dumpster."

"Well, I don't even remember that. I just remember the pool hall."

"Right." A sudden thought occurs to the Operator and he stands up from the wall. "Who sent you?"

"The Enforcers."

"Then why do they want you dead?"

"I don't know."

The Operator paces. Lucy puts her elbows on her knees, forehead in her hands.

"Was your team going to get on board?" the Operator says.

Lucy nods in her hands. "That was the plan. Infiltrate the ship."

"And did you even get close?"

Lucy shakes her head no, then says, "No," with disappointment heavy in her voice.

"No wonder you can shoot. And fight," the Operator says, thinking out loud.

Lucy shrugs.

The Operator looks at the despondent Lucy, wondering what Miguel would say and do. He walks over to the staircase and sits down next to her. He decides Miguel would put his arm around her, but that's not his style. Instead, he looks at the wall ahead of them.

"Sorry about your team," he says, surprised about how much he means it.

"It's okay."

"No, it's not. Losing someone is never easy." The Operator thinks about Fenix, the dog that became his best friend. They were together in the badlands, on his return to the city, but he couldn't survive a bullet from Bacas.

The pair sit in silence, each one lost in their own painful memories.

"What are we going to do?" Lucy says after some time, still looking at the ground.

"Well, the first thing we have to do is keep you safe. The entire city is looking for you right now."

CHAPTER THIRTEEN

THE OPERATOR and Lucy stare at Chance's entrance from the shadows between two buildings across the street. There's nobody in line, and no bouncer at the door.

"Are you sure it's there?" Lucy asks.

"Positive."

"Guess we don't have to worry about the crowds then."

The Operator steps forward and peeks out into the street, looking both ways while searching for Sigma residents on the hunt. Seeing none, he waves Lucy forward. They walk across the street, standing tall and walking at a typical speed so that anyone who might see them doesn't get suspicious. Aggressive bass spills from the nightclub as they approach. The Operator pulls the front door open for Lucy when they get to the entrance, checking for Sigma residents one last time before plunging into the darkness.

A bouncer sits on a stool just inside the front door, his large frame dwarfing his seat. He waves in both Lucy and the Operator without thinking before recognition spreads over the man's face when he realizes the fugitive woman just walked past him.

Surprised, he then recognizes the Operator from the last time he was there, when he took a bouncer hostage behind the bar.

Lucy walks into the club through the double doors while the bouncer reaches out and grabs the Operator's arm.

"You here to cause trouble again?" the bouncer snarls.

The Operator looks at the hand grabbing him then rips his arm away. The bouncer's grip is powerful but no match for the sudden movement; the stool tips forward and he puts heavy feet down so he doesn't fall over.

"Need to see Pavlova," the Operator says.

The bouncer smiles, displaying an impressive array of sharpened teeth, the bottom row covered in gold. "Not sure even he can help you," the bouncer says.

"I'll see what he has to say about that."

The Operator follows Lucy into the club. The music is as loud as the Operator remembers. It reverberates through his skeleton and he feels the bass in his teeth. Lucy looks around in awe, taking in the neon-colored lights on the walls and ceiling, reminiscent of the flashing billboards high above the surface. The air is thick, like someone cranked up the haze from outside and condensed it inside the space. The few people inside dance as if the place is packed, clustered in front of massive speakers on the far wall while pulsing lights flash above and in front of them.

Foregoing words, the Operator taps Lucy's arm and nods towards the bar on their right. The bartender's eyes widen when she sees the Operator, but she continues on as if she doesn't recognize him.

"What will it be?" she says. It's the same bartender who reported him to the bouncers when he asked about acquiring a blaster.

"Two Serums," the Operator says, holding up two fingers.

The bartender pours their drinks and sets them down on the bar.

"Tell Pavlova I want to see him," the Operator says before grabbing his drink.

The bartender sets her jaw and nods before walking away.

The pair turn around. The Operator takes a sip of his drink. Lucy stares at hers.

"One's not going to do anything. It doesn't have much of an effect on us," the Operator says, referring to how they're both androids.

Lucy sniffs the drink then takes a sip. "It's not that good," she says.

The Operator chuckles. "Helps calm the nerves," he says before taking a sip.

Together they watch the dancing group in front of the speakers. The flashing light pulsates in time with the music's beat. Sweat covers the dancers' faces, their hair and shirts sticking to their skin.

"They're having a good time," Lucy says while they wait.

The bartender taps the Operator's shoulder when she returns. "He's busy right now but he said he'll be down as soon as he's free."

"Where is everyone?" the Operator asks.

"It's early," the bartender says. "It'll get busier later on. Or, it should. Not exactly a normal night," she says, nodding towards Lucy.

"Why isn't tonight a normal night?" Lucy asks, missing the gesture.

"Because everyone's busy looking for you."

Lucy sets down her drink and pulls the Operator away from the bartender.

"We should get out of here," she says.

"Where else would we go?" the Operator says, out of ideas.

Lucy looks at the wound on the Operator's side and the dust on his face. "I don't know," she admits, defeated.

"Pavlova's got connections all over the city. He wouldn't risk them by helping Jirasek." When Lucy doesn't say anything, he adds, "I think."

The pair take their drinks and stand near a door in the back of the club, facing the entrance while they wait for Pavlova. Three adventurous dancers approach and try dancing with them, but a stern look from the Operator sends them back to their cluster. He finishes his drink in two large gulps and takes his glass back to the bar before returning to Lucy's side while she nurses her Serum.

A bouncer emerges from the door they stand near, closes it, and stations himself in front of it. Then, two more bouncers take posts on each side of the main entrance and one emerges from the door behind the bar. When the Operator catches the bartender glancing at him, she turns her head away and busies herself with cleaning the glasses.

Pavlova shows up after a prolonged wait. He storms through the front entrance, his eyes searching. Finding the Operator and Lucy, he walks towards them with long, purposeful strides, extending his hand when he gets to them.

"I'd say it's good to see you again, but I'd be lying," he says, yelling over the music, as he shakes the Operator's hand. He's dressed in his usual black suit, shirt, tie, and shoes. His hair is longer than when the Operator last saw him, slicked back against his scalp.

"And you. I've seen your face but haven't had the pleasure," he says, addressing Lucy.

Lucy looks at the Operator, who shrugs. "Lucy," she says, placing her hand in Pavlova's. He takes it and kisses it.

"Let's go to my office—we can talk there." Pavlova looks at the bouncer guarding the back door, who bends over, withdraws a key hanging from his neck from beneath his shirt, and opens it right away. Then, Pavlova leads them down an empty hallway with concrete walls, his footsteps clicking against the concrete floor. Somehow, he walks in time with the music.

"In here," Pavlova says, holding the door open for Lucy. He walks in behind her, cutting off the Operator. There's a desk on the far wall, with curtains behind it that the Operator suspects cover up more concrete. Pavlova ushers Lucy to a plush red couch and takes a seat next to her after she sits. The Operator sits on a matching chair also surrounding a mahogany coffee table.

"Oh! Where are my manners. Anything to drink?" he says to Lucy.

"No, thank you," she replies.

He doesn't ask the Operator.

Pavlova leans back, puts the arm closest to Lucy around the back of the couch, and crosses his left leg over his right. "You two have been *busy*."

"What do you mean?" the Operator asks, his eyes narrowing.

"Well, I heard all about your little run-in with the Dominguez brothers. Apparently, Nacho told them that I said you were off-limits! I wonder how that happened."

"Ask Nacho," the Operator says.

"Well, I've been busy talking to the angry one, trying to keep him from coming after me too. You really shouldn't have broken into their garage—"

"People were chasing her!"

"Or stolen their hovercraft—"

"We had to get away!"

Pavlova laughs while standing up. He looks at Lucy. "Are you sure you don't want anything? I'm going to have a drink myself. Don't make me drink alone!"

The Operator closes his eyes and exhales through his nose, calming himself. "Look, we need help keeping her safe."

"I figured as much," Pavlova says while pouring Serum from a crystal decanter. He sits back down with his drink in hand. "But I'm going to need something from you in return."

"Of course you do," the Operator says, crossing his arms while leaning back in his own seat. "What is it?"

"The Dominguez brothers. Well, brother." Pavlova leans forward and sets his glass on the coffee table so he can use both hands while talking. "Look, I understand he's upset. But I couldn't let him get away with accusing me of something I never did and calling me names."

The Operator tilts his head, his eyebrows meeting above his nose.

"Long story short, I need you to get rid of him."

The Operator sighs. "We don't have time for this."

"Doesn't sound like you have any other options," Pavlova says, picking his glass back up and taking a long drink.

"Will you keep her safe?" the Operator says.

"Oh, that's not up to me. That depends on you." Pavlova's eyes twinkle with mischief.

"On if I take out the brother?"

"And whoever else he brings."

"Brings? Brings where?"

"Here! I told them you're here, with her, and he said something about revenge against us both. They should be here soon."

The Operator sits bolt upright. Lucy stands up.

"Sit down," Pavlova says. "We'll be working together! I'm not going to let some upstart street racer insult me and get away with it."

Lucy meets the Operator's eyes, asking what they'll do without saying a word.

"Don't really have much of a choice, do we," the Operator says, his voice not much louder than a whisper.

"Not really. You don't help us defend the place, I'll just hand her over to Jirasek myself."

"Nobody will listen to some surface-dweller that high up," the Operator says.

Pavlova beams with pride when he hears the Operator's description of himself. "Oh, I wouldn't go," he says, laughing. "You think I'd give all this up? Sigma's practically mine. No, I'd send someone else, extend my eyes and ears even further," he says, opening his eyes wide. He turns to Lucy. "Nobody appreciates the value of information anymore," he says, feigning sadness.

Someone knocks at the door. "Come in," Pavlova says.

It's the bouncer that the Operator shot the last time he was in the club. There's an unmistakable look of disgust on the man's face when he recognizes Pavlova's guest, but no surprise—word travels fast.

"They're gathering outside," the bouncer says.

"Took them long enough!"

When the bouncer doesn't leave, Pavlova looks at him and asks if there's anything else. "We're helping this guy *again?*" the bouncer asks without hiding his displeasure.

"You just do what I say, and I'll make sure your family stays fed," Pavlova responds.

The bouncer's tough demeanor crumbles at the mention of his family. "Yes, sir," he says, withdrawing from the room. "Thank you," he adds, before disappearing.

"Good help is so hard to find these days."

"Everyone would've found out eventually, wouldn't they?" Lucy says to Pavlova, the most words she's spoken since they arrived in his office.

Pavlova looks at her with a mixture of pride and sadness.

"Unfortunately, yes. There's no hiding that face—it's been pasted all over the city."

"Better to let them come when we're prepared than wait and hope and wonder," Lucy continues, thinking out loud.

"More or less, yes."

"And if we're already here causing headaches, might as well get us in on the fight too," she says.

"Nothing for free in this world," Pavlova says, tapping his nose. "And we can remind the Dominguez brothers who runs things in this district. Their heads have been getting a bit too big for my liking lately. You know they stole my favorite hovercraft? Her name was Charlotte: a Hyperling Motors special edition. Dark red, customized interior—they kept denying they had it but I know it was them."

The Operator and Lucy meet each other's eyes and turn away.

"You didn't happen to see it in their garage, did you?"

The Operator looks up out of the corner of his eyes as if he's imagining the garage's layout. Then, he scrunches his face and shakes his head. "No, I don't remember seeing it."

"Maybe after all this you can show me where their garage is and I'll have a look myself. I'll take two if they don't have it."

An explosion rocks the nightclub. The Operator grabs on to each side of the chair. He looks over at the couch and finds Lucy with her hands on the cushions, bracing herself. Pavlova smiles and takes a sip of his drink.

"Better get out there before they overrun my men," he says with a smirk.

CHAPTER FOURTEEN

The Operator and Lucy run from the office, pass the locked door that leads to the rear of the dance floor, and continue down the hall into the lounge area behind the bar. A folding metal barrier sits just inside the red-walled room. Four large chairs and a coffee table sit against the wall farthest away from the bar, below the wide mirror, leaving the center of the room open beneath a crystal chandelier. Two bouncers carrying blaster rifles pointed at the ground wave the pair through, urging them forward to the door that leads to the bar, knowing the two androids are on their side.

Pausing outside the door behind the bar, the Operator pulls his blaster from its holster and listens. There's shouting from the other side—Pavlova's team preparing their defenses. He doesn't hear any shots. He looks at Lucy and her empty hands.

"You don't have a blaster—"

Lucy shakes her head.

Looking at the two bouncers guarding the entrance to the hall, the Operator notices one has a blaster pistol sidearm. "Give it to her," he says, pointing to the weapon.

The bouncer looks down at his side then back to the Operator. "No, it's mine!" he says in anger.

"Then give her the rifle."

His anger turns to trepidation. He glances at his partner, both of them behind the metal barrier, and the second man shrugs.

"Can't. Rifle belongs to Pavlova."

"Then give her the gun," the second bouncer says, gesturing with his head towards Lucy.

The hesitant bouncer with the blaster pistol sets his jaw and withdraws the sidearm. As Lucy walks over, he lets the handle fall, the weapon supported by his finger in the trigger guard.

"I'll make sure you get it back," Lucy says, taking the blaster.

"Sure," the bouncer grumbles.

The Operator looks at the blaster when Lucy gets back to his side. "Good enough in a pinch," he says, giving her a nod. She shrugs and returns the gesture. He pushes the swinging door open and emerges into the club.

The lights are on, four bright bulbs in the four corners of the room that cut through the manufactured haze. The flashing lights that created the atmosphere continue pulsing, though they can't match the overhead light's intensity and become part of the background. Without the haze and dim lighting, the neon graffiti looks like the work of an amateur. The partiers huddle in a corner, sitting together in a tight cluster. Some of them look terrified, their eyes glossy as they stare at the club's defenders moving about the room, and some continue moving to the music in their head, gyrating while seated.

There are a series of foldable metal barriers set up throughout the dance floor, arranged in an alternating pattern of twos and threes facing the entrance. In addition to the bouncers —more of which materialized while the Operator and Lucy were in Pavlova's office—a number of skinless androids wait behind the barriers with their blaster rifles resting on the top edge. Two bouncers with thick metal clubs stand on either side of the front door; the tiny stool sat on by the bouncer that let them in is behind the one on the left.

The Operator and Lucy set up behind the bar, next to the bartender. She has a modified shotgun resting on the bar, aimed at the door. The wooden stock stands in stark contrast to the shimmering metal barrel crisscrossed with neon tubes—a mixture of ancient and modern technology.

"Old-school ammo or energy?" the Operator asks.

The bartender pulls her gaze away from the entrance and gives the Operator a proud grin. "Energy. Designed it myself."

The Operator nods his approval.

Another explosion outside rattles the front door. The Operator and Lucy rest their arms on the bar, their blasters pointed at the door, while war cries from outside trickle in, variations of demands for Lucy and denouncements against Pavlova for harboring her.

"Most of them are human," Lucy whispers to the Operator while the crowd outside works themselves into a frenzy.

The Operator looks out at the dance floor covered with defenders. Confused, he says, "There's a good bit of androids—"

"No, outside. The ones trying to get in. Sigma's residents."

"Oh. Yes, they're all human. No androids this far down." Aware of the androids set up behind the barriers, as well as himself and Lucy, he adds, "Well, no androids out there."

"And we're going to just shoot them?"

"Do you know any other way to get rid of an angry mob?" the bartender asks. When Lucy doesn't respond, she shrugs. "Can't just go storming into people's place of business."

The doors start rattling and everyone's attention turns towards the club's entrance. "Don't take any chances," the bartender mutters under her breath.

The Operator wonders if she said the club's name on purpose.

The bouncers on each side of the front door widen their stance, their metal clubs held back at chest height. Every person in the club stares at the front door, waiting in silence. All of a sudden, music starts blaring from the speakers. Startled, everyone turns around and looks at the source of the noise. One of the partiers, his eyes wide open and sweat dripping from his stringy hair, starts bobbing his head in time with the beat until a skinless android close by shoots him in the chest.

The doors burst open and a flood of people storm through the entrance. The distracted bouncers on each side of the entrance swing their clubs too late. Their strikes find the faces of the first infiltrators but they don't have time for another swing before the mass of bodies overruns them. Everyone in the room empties their clip into the crowd.

As the Sigma residents fall, the Operator sees them drop small metal balls. Dozens hit the ground. Some are silver, some jet black, and at least two are bright green. As soon as the realization hits, the Operator stops shooting, grabs Lucy, and pulls her down behind the bar.

Explosions rock the room. Shrapnel hits every surface, striking the wall behind the bar as well as the bartender. She goes down in a heap, her face covered with small holes.

The Operator peeks his head over the bar. Large craters cover the ground near the entrance, and plumes of dark green gas surround the two nearby bouncers—they writhe on the ground, their hands around their throats. As the Operator watches, a hovercraft backs up to the front of the club and revs its engine. The exhaust pushes the poisonous gas farther into Chance. The nearest androids are unresponsive, decimated by the shrapnel and explosions, but those stationed farther back, still moving on the ground, show no signs that the poison gas affects them.

A thickset man in a gas mask pushes two young men into the club, his face emerging into the room for a moment before disappearing back to safety. The vanguard bury their faces into the collar of their shirts and run into the space, falling onto all fours when they get inside. They crawl forward and take up position behind the twisted metal barriers closest to the door. The Operator watches their faces emerge from behind their shirts. They take a few tentative breaths and make sour faces before giving the man a thumbs-up. Then, the man in a gas mask steps into the club and makes a low sweeping motion with his arms, unleashing another wave of Sigma residents into the space. They rush in with the music blaring and bass reverberating throughout the room, blocking the man in the gas mask from view.

The androids in the back of the room, still functional after the surprise attack, shoot everyone they can, eliminating those in front. The surviving residents take cover behind the metal barriers that survived the explosions.

Instead of firing on the Sigma residents, the Operator watches the front door, waiting for a shot on the man wearing a gas mask. Lucy doesn't shoot anyone.

A barrage of fire from still more residents at the entrance pins the androids down behind their barriers. They huddle with their backs to the metal, waiting. The bartender groans and Lucy drops down behind the bar.

"She's alive," Lucy says to the Operator. He doesn't take his eyes from the front door. The shooters stream inside while Lucy starts dragging the bartender towards the swinging door and the lounge beyond.

One of the partiers, his jerky movements betraying the substance coursing through his veins, stands up and runs towards the front door with a scream. The man in the gas mask walks away from the crowd so he can meet the fleeing man, leveling him with a savage blow to his face.

Seeing his opportunity, the Operator fires. The shot hits the leader in the head; he stumbles but doesn't fall. The clear, hard material surrounding his head has spiderweb cracks along the surface, including in front of his eyes. While the Operator watches, the man pulls the protective casing from around his head, which also pulls the gas mask away from in front of his face. The stocky Dominguez brother, his eyes wide with adrenaline and rage, turns and looks at the Operator behind the bar. He pulls a vial from his pocket and slams it into his forearm: Stim.

Before the Operator can fire again, the shooters laying down cover fire turn their attention away from the pinned-down androids and towards him, lighting up the bar's front and the wall behind. He ducks down before any of the shots can find their mark. Annoyed that the protective helmet stopped the shot to the Dominguez brother's head, the Operator begins crawling towards the swinging door Lucy disappeared behind with the bartender.

"Thought you could pick me off, huh!" the stocky Dominguez brother yells out. "Like I'd come in here without protection!"

The Operator passes through the door and stands up once he's well inside the lounge. There are more barriers spaced out in the room, manned by more skinless androids and bouncers. The Operator sees Lucy dragging the bartender down the hall on the far side of the lounge and weaves through the erected defenses on his way to her.

"She should be fine," Pavlova says while leaning into the hall from his office and inspecting the bartender on the ground. He looks at the Operator. "You should be helping get rid of the intruders. They take over the place, she's gone," he says, pointing to Lucy as he turns away.

Someone bangs against the locked door that leads into the hallway from the dance floor. A moment later, there's another loud crash that sounds like a thrown shoulder.

Lucy continues dragging the bartender to Pavlova's office, despite the owner's dismissive attitude. The Operator walks around the pair and gets to the office first. "How sturdy is that door?" the Operator asks.

Pavlova laughs. "Nobody's getting through that. They'd have better luck taking out the whole wall."

An explosion from behind the locked door rocks the room. Pavlova smiles when he sees the Operator flinch. "Like I said, that'll take the wall down before that door."

Pavlova looks at the computer at his desk. "Well, that's interesting."

"What?" the Operator says, looking back down the hall at a stream of Sigma residents in the lounge meeting a wall of bullets after they storm through the swinging doors.

"Hector's the only one on the other side of that door," Pavlova says. "Sure is a lot of noise for one man."

The Operator turns back to Pavlova. "You sure it's just him?"

"Positive," Pavlova says, nodding with his lips sealed shut.

The Operator, his blaster in hand, approaches the locked door as Lucy pulls the bartender into Pavlova's office. He puts his head against the door and listens. There's a loud slam on the other side the second he looks down at the floor. Startled but unmoving, he keeps listening and hears the slow, retreating footsteps. Then, the footsteps quicken on their approach. The Operator opens the door when he thinks that Hector Dominguez will strike it again.

He's late. Instead of the man's momentum carrying him

straight through to the hallway's wall, the man hits the door first, then is almost standing tall when the door opens. The Operator planned on shutting the door as soon as Hector came inside, making sure nobody else got behind their defenses but the leader. Instead, the Operator pulls Hector through, forgetting about his blaster when closing the door becomes his primary focus.

The stocky Dominguez brother almost resists falling forward, but when he does crash through the threshold he takes the Operator down with him. The defenders in the lounge still have their back turned and don't know about the open door behind them.

Both men fight for the door—Hector wanting it open, the Operator wanting it closed. The Operator, on top of Hector at first, tries reaching for the door, but Hector grabs his leg and pulls him away. Hector then gets on top of the Operator, taking his back. The Operator stands up with the added weight and tries walking to the door. The wound in his side screams from the pressure. Hector leans back, his arms around the Operator's neck. The Operator gives in to the momentum and slams Hector into the wall behind them. The Stimmed man doesn't release his hold. Then, the Operator stands tall and jumps backwards while orienting himself horizontal, landing with his full force on top of Hector. The air leaves Hector's lungs and he releases his grip.

The Operator scrambles off Hector and reaches for the door. He wraps his fingers around the edge and pulls it hard, but it doesn't close—Hector's foot is in the way. The Operator crawls towards the last bit of open space between the door and the wall and tries pushing Hector's leg away. Hector grabs a hold of his shoulders and pulls him back to the floor.

Then, Hector rolls himself on top of the Operator, sitting on the Operator's chest. He begins raining blows on the Operator's face, putting the entirety of his weight behind the strikes.

All of a sudden, Hector's face disappears in a rain of gore and he falls forward. His stomach hits the Operator's battered face. The Operator throws the man off of him, still worried about closing the door.

When the world around the Operator reappears, he sees Lucy with a blaster in her hand walking from Pavlova's office to the door leading to the back of the club. With her left hand on the door, she fires two quick shots into the club with the blaster in her right without any change in her expression. She closes the door with a gentle push. The Operator hears two bodies hit the floor before the door clicks shut.

Her face still an expressionless mask, Lucy walks towards the lounge and starts firing.

CHAPTER FIFTEEN

"WHAT HAPPENED?" Lucy asks the Operator as he lowers the blaster pistol she had aimed at the entrance with his hand. They're in the middle of the dance floor surrounded by the bodies of bouncers, skinless androids, and Sigma residents.

"You protected the club," the Operator whispers. There's a deep cut over his right eye, and his nose feels out of place.

Lucy looks at the bodies around her with wide eyes. Startled, she drops the blaster and starts backing away. A single shot rings out from the fallen blaster, hitting the wall. The cement crumbles and more of the graffiti adorning it falls away. She bumps into one of the metal barriers that escaped destruction, jumping at the touch.

"What have I done?" she whispers to herself, her words getting caught in her throat. She turns to the Operator and wraps her arms around him, burying her face in his neck.

"You did what you had to do," the Operator says. He pats her back before prying her off of him.

One of Pavlova's bouncers and two skinless androids pick a mangled door from the ground and lean it against the entrance. They usher the surviving partygoers from the room with a shove, the bouncer telling them, "Chance is closed until further notice," before placing a second door next to the first. They start piling available scrap against the doors: folding metal barriers, destroyed speakers, and inert skinless androids.

"They can stay there for now," the bouncer says when he sees Lucy's horrified expression.

Clapping rings out from the back of the dance floor. Pavlova appears from the door leading into the hallway. "Now *that* was impressive," he says.

Lucy shakes her head as if the words hurt her ears.

Pavlova approaches the pair. He puts a hand on Lucy's shoulder. "There's nothing to be ashamed of! You were just doing what you're programmed to do," the club owner says.

Lucy pulls away from Pavlova's touch. "I killed them," she says.

"And what did you think they were going to do to you? Send you to Jirasek for a cup of tea? You saved yourself, and your friends," Pavlova says, opening his arms wide and gesturing to the surrounding space.

The Operator bends down and picks up the dropped blaster. "Let's get this back to its owner," he says.

Pavlova swipes at the air. "Don't worry about that, he'll be fine without it. Keep it; you earned it!"

Lucy gives Pavlova a poisonous stare. "I said I'd give it back."

"Suit yourself," Pavlova says, walking away from the pair and inspecting the growing pile in front of the club's entrance.

The Operator and Lucy walk around the bar and into the lounge behind. There's a group of bouncers huddled together next to their fallen comrades, the bodies arranged shoulder to shoulder on the floor next to shattered crystals from the chandelier. The invading Sigma residents still lie where they fell.

When Lucy finds the man the blaster belonged to among

the bodies, she freezes in place; her shoulders fall and she hangs her head.

The Operator, putting his nose back in place using the large mirror on the wall, speaks to Lucy through the reflection. "Guess it's yours now," he says. He turns around and holds the blaster out.

"You're a better shot anyways," one of the men says with a chuckle, a weak attempt at a joke. The rest of the bouncers manage a quick spurt of forced laughter before the situation's solemnity takes over again.

Lucy accepts the blaster with a solemn nod, as if the weapon is a relic honoring every fallen man's sacrifice. The Operator puts a hand on Lucy's lower back, ushering her away from the carnage. Together, they walk through the back hallway and into Pavlova's office, where they find the injured bartender lying on his couch. Her breathing is shallow but regular, her face a bloody mess.

The Operator pokes his head back into the hallway and yells to the bouncers in the lounge. "Got an injured one in here!"

Two bouncers leave the lounge and walk to the office. One of them picks up the bartender, saying he'll take her to her family himself. The other bouncer looks at the Operator and a distraught Lucy. "Her dad's a doctor; he'll know what to do."

The Operator and Lucy collapse into the two chairs facing the couch. There's a dark stain on the red sofa where the bartender's head rested moments before. They sit in silence while everyone else scurries around the club recovering from the attack.

After a while, they hear Pavlova coming down the hall, barking a list of orders. "Once they fix the doors, tell them to get started replacing the flooring. Another team can start with the bar."

Pavlova appears in the office, a skinless android following him. "And what about the walls? Should we get a local artist in here to redo the artwork?" the skinless android says.

"No, the walls can stay the way they are. It's a good reminder for everyone about what happens when you try attacking me." Pavlova starts walking towards the couch but changes his mind when he sees the bloodstain. Instead, he walks around his desk.

"Anything else?" the skinless android asks, standing on the opposite side of the desk.

"A new couch."

"Got it. I'll get everything started right away," the android says, turning around.

"I want this place back open for tomorrow night," Pavlova says to the android's back.

The android's head turns around, but their body continues forward. "We won't stop working until it's done."

Pavlova nods once and sits down. "Well, that was unpleasant," he says.

The Operator nods. Lucy stares at the bloodstain on the couch.

"We should all get some rest," Pavlova says. "I'd offer you a place to stay in the next building but I can't protect you there."

"We're fine staying here," the Operator says. There's no sign Lucy even registers their conversation.

"We can clear out some space in our storage room. Not very comfortable, but at least it's safe."

Pavlova looks around his desk as if he's looking for another conversation topic. Finding none, he taps the desk twice and stands up. "Yes, let's go get you situated."

The storage room is a small room attached to the back of the lounge behind the bar. The bodies are gone from the lounge but there are still bloodstains on the ground from where both Sigma residents and bouncers fell. While the Operator walks through, he thinks about Lucy's efficient suppression of the invasion.

After she left the Operator's side, she walked into the lounge standing tall. Before any of the Sigma residents knew what was going on, she fired a series of shots into where the chandelier hung from the ceiling, dropping the fixture onto their heads. She picked up a dropped blaster rifle with her left hand and held it at her hip. The Sigma residents who escaped from the falling chandelier jumped back, exposing themselves—Lucy made them pay for their mistake with blaster fire from both weapons. By that point, the Operator was behind her, and he followed her into the club through the swinging door behind the bar.

Lucy walked straight at the back door Hector came through without any regard for her own safety, firing a flurry of shots into two more Sigma residents who were attempting a flanking attack. The Operator, looking into the club from a crouched position with just his eyes above the bar, took out four men who ran in and aimed at Lucy but didn't see him with four quick shots. She turned towards the dance floor with a snarl when she heard the men drop. She marched forward, into the center of the club, and shot every Sigma resident turning the corner into Chance, accumulating a massive pile of bodies outside the entrance. She dropped the blaster rifle when it jammed, continuing her stand with just her pistol.

By the time Lucy realized what she was doing, nobody dared enter the club—the surviving Sigma residents pulled the bodies of their comrades back by the legs, making sure they weren't exposed to the shooter within the space.

"You can make a pile with the boxes in the back of the room; that should give you two enough space," Pavlova says.

The Operator blinks three times, coming back from his memory to the present.

"Did you hear me? I said make a pile. I'm not doing it myself," Pavlova says with a chuckle while shaking his head.

"I heard you," the Operator says. He looks at Lucy. "I'll get it set up."

Lucy nods.

The Operator walks into the room—little more than a large closet—and starts rearranging the boxes, maximizing open floor space.

"I'll be back in the morning," Pavlova says, turning away.

An out-of-breath bouncer storms into the lounge from the hallway; it's the same one who took the bartender back to her family. "I've been looking for you, sir," he says to Pavlova.

"What is it?"

"The residents. They're . . . They're forming teams, deciding the best course of action. Some want another attack."

The Operator sets down a box of liquor against the back wall at chest height and turns around. He watches as Lucy's faraway gaze turns to sadness.

"They're coming back already?" Pavlova says. He looks at the Operator. "Might want to hold off on that," he says, pointing to the boxes.

The Operator crosses his arms and leans against the door's threshold, waiting.

"Well, that's the thing. They can't agree, and they have started fighting among themselves about what they should do. I was sneaking by when I heard the first shots ring out."

"They're shooting each other now?" Pavlova says, laughing. "This is too perfect. Good, let them shoot themselves, less for us to deal with if they come for her again."

Lucy walks into the storage room and sits down, hugging her knees with her back against a stack of boxes.

"We need to rest," the Operator says. "Come get us if they start attacking the club."

"Oh, we will. She'll make quick work of anyone trying to mess with us again," Pavlova says with a wink, gesturing with his chin to Lucy.

The Operator shuts the door on Pavlova and the bouncer. He hears them walking away while he clears enough room for both him and Lucy on the ground. Lucy doesn't move. When he finishes, he lies down on the floor, his hands over his chest. He closes his eyes.

"I'm going to give myself up," Lucy says.

The Operator takes a deep breath and lets it trickle out through his nose. "What makes you say that?"

"Did you see all of the dead Sigma residents? And now, more are dying! All because of me."

"It's because of Jirasek, not you."

"Nobody else has to die. I'll just turn myself in. You can take the prize."

The Operator laughs. "You think Pavlova will let me take that trip? I don't want it anyways. The upper levels and me . . . we don't get along."

"Fine, Pavlova can have the prize. Either way, no more Sigma residents have to die."

The Operator rolls onto his elbow and props himself up with a sigh. "Look, they made their decision. They want to risk their life for a chance at the seventy-fourth? Fine. That's their choice. But you didn't make them do it, and you're not to blame."

"I killed them. And the worst part? I don't even remember doing it."

"Then what's the problem? Go to sleep, you'll feel better in the morning."

"The problem is that I know they're out there, fighting amongst themselves because of me! Gamma's market got destroyed, now Sigma is fighting—destruction follows me wherever I go." Lucy rests her forehead against her knees and takes deep, rattling breaths. "I can't live with it. I wish I'd never woken up, just stayed a thoughtless android."

The Operator reaches out and grabs her lower leg, shaking her. "Look, we'll figure this out. Just don't give up."

"What else can we do? There's nowhere to go, Jirasek made sure the entire city is off-limits."

"We could leave the city." The Operator never realized how important staying in the city is to him until the words leave his lips.

To his surprised relief, she shakes her head no. "I'm tired of running."

The Operator drops his gaze while he thinks. "Then why don't we fight?"

Lucy lifts her head and looks at him with stern eyes. "I'm not killing anyone else."

"Not even Jirasek?"

CHAPTER SIXTEEN

THE NEXT MORNING, Pavlova's lips curl downwards when he hears the Operator and Lucy plan on taking down Jirasek. He's sitting at his desk across from the Operator, with a plate of half-eaten eggs next to his computer. Lucy stayed in the storage room, saying she needed some time alone.

"It's perfect. If we're not here, the Sigma residents won't have any more reason to keep fighting. And you don't have to worry about protecting your club anymore!" the Operator says.

Pavlova rests his elbows on the desk and steeples his hands. "And why would I help you? You showed up, I got my club destroyed, and then you leave. What do I get out of this?"

The Operator leans back in his chair. "The attack wasn't a complete waste. You got rid of one of the Dominguez brothers, and showed everyone who's in charge of the district."

"Well, now the other one's going to come after me."

"With who? Sigma's not ready for another fight. They're still fighting amongst themselves, right?"

"As far as I know."

"So there's nothing to worry about until they sort themselves out—who knows how long that will take. And, once we take down Jirasek, the entire city will open back up again. Stealing hovercrafts for the street races will be back on the table."

It's Pavlova's turn to lean back in his chair. He looks at the ceiling, thinking. "He won't forget about Hector's death."

"Make sure he doesn't! That's what happens when you cross Regulo Pavlova."

Pavlova turns his gaze from the ceiling to the Operator and smiles. "That's a good point." His eyes shift to the left while he continues thinking. "Getting to Jirasek's ship won't be easy . . ."

The Operator tells Pavlova about Lucy's initial mission, how she was part of a squadron sent by the Enforcers tasked with boarding the ship and taking it down.

"See? Even they couldn't get onto the ship."

"We'll figure something out. But we can't do it from down here . . ."

"And you need my help getting to the upper levels," Pavlova says with a sigh. "There's always a catch."

The Operator shrugs, accompanied by a slight head nod.

Pavlova turns to his computer and starts typing. "Give me some time. I'll come get you when I figure something out."

The Operator goes back to the liquor storage room where he spent the previous night and finds Lucy hasn't moved an inch while he was gone. He turns the lights on and she continues staring at the ceiling, unblinking. He sits down on the floor with his back against a stack of boxes. "Pavlova's agreed to help us," he says.

"That's good."

"We'll get to the upper levels and figure out a way onto the ship."

"Our team was *made* to get onto the ship. If we couldn't do it, what hope do the two of us have?"

The Operator nods. "Well, we have to try. You said yourself that you're tired of running."

"I am."

"Then we don't really have any other choice."

Lucy takes a deep breath and sits up. "So, we just wait until Pavlova sends us away?"

"We could. Or, we can help them rebuild."

Lucy nods, and the Operator helps her stand up. Together, they walk out to the dance floor and ask the skinless android in charge how they can help.

"You can help repair the front doors. Keep your blasters ready in case anyone from Sigma tries to get in."

The Operator and Lucy become part of the team holding up the new, thicker metal doors. They keep one hand on the door, the other free in case they need their weapon. Occasional gunfire and explosions ring out in the distance, none of them close enough for alarm. The Operator looks at Lucy, worried that she'll think about the human cost of the created factions. Her expression doesn't change.

After the installation of the new doors, the skinless android in charge tasks them with cleaning the burn marks and poison gas residue from the nearby walls. All the human bouncers clear the area before they get to work, far away from the fumes. Scrubbing the walls with a coarse sponge creates a consistent scratching that limits all but the loudest sounds from outside. The pair don't talk while they work for hours, clearing away both the new stains and years of old residue from countless nights of smoky haze.

Early in the afternoon, a human bouncer calls to the Operator and Lucy from behind the bar. They stop their work and turn around.

"Just wanted to let you know that Ramona's goin' to be all right. Just got word from her folks."

The Operator nods. Lucy exhales a sigh before thanking the bouncer for letting her know and turning back to her work.

"She said to tell you thanks," the bouncer adds before walking back into the lounge.

There's a noticeable change in Lucy's demeanor after hearing about the bartender's prognosis. Instead of hearing the sounds of faraway battles among the Sigma residents and staring ahead expressionless, she shakes her head in sadness.

"Don't they realize Jirasek only offered *one* spot on the upper levels?" she says after a rapid series of gunfire close to the club.

"I don't think it's about that anymore. It's turned into a fight for supremacy in Sigma."

"And we're sitting here at ground zero."

"It's ground zero because you're sitting here."

Lucy chuckles and shakes her head again.

They aren't back to work very long before Pavlova calls to them from the door at the back of the club. "Leave that for someone else and get back here!" he says.

The Operator and Lucy walk around the dance floor's perimeter while a team of skinless androids replaces the flooring. They climb over the massive speakers on the exposed ground at the back of the club, then go through the door and into Pavlova's office. They sit down in front of his desk while he closes the door behind them.

"I've got something," Pavlova says with excitement, taking his seat on the opposite side of the desk. "You said she tried getting onto the ship with an elite team, right?"

Lucy glares at the Operator. "You told him?"

"Yes, but it doesn't matter. Look, if they couldn't get on board, it's not looking great for the two of you."

The Operator opens his mouth, but Pavlova's raised hand stops him from speaking.

"So, I thought we need to work smarter, not harder." Pavlova continues when the Operator and Lucy don't say a word. "The ship runs on Jirasek's private network, which is based in Jirasek Tower. If we could take over the network and disable it, none of the ship's defenses will work."

"Did your team try that?" the Operator asks Lucy.

Lucy looks down at her knees. "I don't remember," she says with a frown. "But if *he* came up with it in less than a day, I'm sure it was a consideration."

"If they didn't go through with it, it's because nobody in the city can do it—except this guy." Pavlova turns his computer monitor around with a dramatic flourish. On the screen is surveillance footage of a young man with a hood and sunglasses outside of what looks like a stall in one of the city's bazaars. "And there's no way he'd *ever* work with Enforcers."

"So why would he work with us?" Lucy asks.

"That's what you need to figure out," Pavlova says, turning his screen back to its original position. "Just don't let him know that you were an Enforcer before your failed mission."

Lucy flexes her jaw at the mention of her squadron's demise.

"Where is he?" the Operator asks.

"At the island resort on the seventy-fourth, living on stolen credits. Everyone knows but nobody can figure out where he got them. I'll get you a better picture so you can identify him."

The Operator sighs. "Even if he agrees to help us, how are we going to get him all the way to Jirasek Tower? Jirasek shoots down everything that flies."

Pavlova smiles. "Jirasek Tower has direct access to the island resort level. Company perk. Get him to the control room and he'll do the rest."

"*If* he agrees to help," Lucy says.

"And *if* we can get up to the seventy-fourth. How are we going to do that?"

Pavlova leans forward in his chair. "Well, I can't get you that high, but I know someone on the forty-second who can." He looks at the Operator with a smirk.

"Who?" Lucy asks, alternating her gaze between Pavlova and the Operator.

"Dr. Howl," the Operator says. "Or, the android who took his face. He's still in charge up there?"

"Nobody's been able to tell," Pavlova says, pleased with himself.

"And how are we going to get there? We can't just fly up."

"Two ropes will be dropping down from the forty-second in"—Pavlova looks at his computer—"twenty minutes. They'll hoist you up. You have until then to get in position."

"Wait, we have to go through the streets?" Lucy asks.

"That's the quickest way," Pavlova says. "There might be a way through adjacent buildings, but I wouldn't count on it. This isn't Gamma."

"How many people will be in our escort?" the Operator says with a sigh. He knows Lucy wants an end to the fighting, but they don't have much of a choice.

Pavlova's laugh is too long and too loud to be real. He slaps the table twice, looks at the Operator, and slaps the table again. "You think I can spare an escort! You two have cost me too many men as it is."

"Too many lives altogether," Lucy whispers.

"So we just walk out the front door and go for a walk to the correct building?" the Operator growls.

Pavlova makes a show of wiping tears from his eyes. "No, no. I wouldn't leave you out in the cold like that. I made a call— the city's top Enforcer is on her way down now."

"Yoshiko?" the Operator asks, incredulous.

"You've heard of her?"

"Something like that." After a pause, the Operator adds, "*She's* our escort?"

Pavlova gives the Operator a look that says he hasn't ever heard anything so foolish in his entire life. "No. I simply reported a team of Jirasek's androids were seen in front of Chance, heading in the direction of the Dominguez brothers' garage."

The Operator never mentioned his run-in with Jirasek's androids in Gamma. He's about to question Pavlova when the club owner continues.

"I guess word got out about our friend here and Jirasek sent his boys down to investigate. They're over by the old train station, but Yoshiko doesn't need to know that."

A skinless android pokes their head into Pavlova's office. "Five Enforcers just dropped in front of the front doors," they say.

Pavlova thanks the android and waves them away. Then, he turns to the Operator and Lucy. "Better get going. Go out the back door at the end of the hall."

He stays seated while the Operator and Lucy start running. They weave through two bouncers in the hallway, unlock a series of bolts and locks, then run through the back door and into a dark alley. The door slams shut behind them.

"This way," the Operator says, running to his right, in the direction away from the train station.

"Do you know where you're going?" Lucy whispers while they inspect the street perpendicular to theirs, looking for movement. Finding none, they start running down the block.

"Somewhat. I know the building, but I don't know which side the ropes will drop down from. We'll have to look for the open port on the forty-second," the Operator says.

At the end of the building, they look at the front of Chance from around the corner and see Yoshiko Apocalypse's team marching away from the club. There are still bodies of Sigma residents piled on each side of the entrance and an assortment of discarded weapons and debris all over the street.

The Operator and Lucy run across the street, continuing on the street parallel to the elite Enforcers. At the end of each block, they make sure the Enforcers pass by the space between buildings before they cross. The sound of gunfire reaches them every so often, followed by a delay in the Enforcer team's progress.

Sigma's residents are gone. Both the Operator and Lucy stay alert as they walk beneath numerous windows and pass countless doors, but there's no movement except for the occasional rat.

Halfway across Sigma, the Operator turns away from the Enforcers, running along a street the team already crossed a block away. Together, he and Lucy jog until the Operator announces they are at the correct building.

It's been twenty minutes since Pavlova's countdown began.

The Operator and Lucy run around the building, their eyes to the sky, when a loud explosion rings out in the distance. "Bet they attacked the Enforcers," the Operator observes, basing his guess on their distance from the sound.

The pair turn the corner, still looking for the open port high above, when headlights flash on ahead of them. The sound of a hovercraft's revving engine pulls the Operator's focus back to the surface, and he pulls Lucy towards the building, away from the vehicle speeding towards them, just in time.

It's the second Dominguez brother. He spins the hovercraft to a stop after missing his targets. He aims at the Operator with the blaster in his hand and a bandage around his head.

The Operator pulls Lucy around the corner in the nick of time. The blaster shot hits the building, taking a chunk from the wall. Two thin black ropes hang down ahead, their bottoms almost touching the surface. They each grab a hold of one and yank.

Their arms almost separate from the force of the ropes' initial pull. They rise up, blowing past the second-level windows and then the reclaimers.

Far below, the surviving Dominguez brother races his hovercraft in a circle around the building, chasing shadows, both revenge and the promise of elevation fueling his search.

CHAPTER SEVENTEEN

THE ROPE STOPS PULLING the Operator and Lucy up the level below the open port. The Operator thinks about the last time he was there, when he fought his way through waves of androids and humans while rescuing Gabi, the young daughter of the doctor who saved his life. Releasing her from imprisonment in the attached science lab, staying behind alone so the transport ship could escape, and fighting the two-gunned android in darkness while members of the Sect engaged in hand-to-hand combat—all because of a debt and a promise.

They climb hand over hand the rest of the way to the port's lip, the massive door looming, half-open, overhead. The ropes rest on each side of a massive crate, one face open to the city air. Two small hovercrafts are parked close to the edge on the far left side of the port.

"Get inside," Dr. Howl says from somewhere close by, within the port. The real Dr. Howl met his demise in the battle for Gabi—this Dr. Howl is a skinless android employed by Pavlova who took the man's face and assumed his role as the city's leading scientist.

The Operator and Lucy climb into the wooden crate. It's

tall enough that they can both stand up but too thin for anything but a sliver of air between them.

"Come over here and take this crate closer to the lab!" Dr. Howl commands, his voice carrying far into the traffic-free city night.

Heavy metal footsteps approach from the center of the port. The sound of hydraulics and metal joints gets louder as the mech suit gets closer.

"Use the pincers," Dr. Howl says. "And tip it forty-five degrees. The back side's open and I don't want my specimen spilling out."

Lucy looks at the Operator with an inquisitive glance. The person operating the mech suit doesn't question the man in charge. "Yes, sir," a husky voice responds.

The Operator and Lucy fall to the back of the wooden crate as the mech suit angles the crate backwards and lifts them up. They stay flat against the back while the mech turns towards the lab, their view shifting from the opposite building's flashing neon billboards to inside the port. The mech suit takes them towards hanging ceiling lights near the wall and the port's upper balconies, a slight bounce with every step it takes.

During their trip, a pair of security guards wearing dark gray compression suits—Dr. Howl's android security team—look at them from the uppermost balcony. As the Operator watches, worried about their discovery, the pair become inert, their heads hanging down against their chest.

The mech orients the crate to vertical once again, bringing the entrance to the science lab into view, before lowering the box containing the Operator and Lucy to the port's floor with a delicate touch.

"That will be all," Dr. Howl says. Following the brusque command, the mech suit turns and walks away.

Dr. Howl's smiling face appears from around the right side

of the crate, complete with his black-rimmed glasses. His hair has a sharp part and is the exact same length as when the Operator last saw him.

He stands in front of the crate, and the Operator discovers the scientist ditched the black overcoat, favoring a simple white button-down shirt with the sleeves rolled up, black tie, and black pants. "Pretend you're controlled by my data pad," Dr. Howl says, holding up a black tablet. He mimes pushing buttons. "And . . . walk," he whispers.

The Operator and Lucy take a few stiff, mechanical steps forward. "More natural. Neither of you look like any of the old models." They both stand tall and walk forward with their heads held high, staring ahead without investigating their surroundings.

A scientist in a white lab coat walks from the science lab. "Sir," she says with a nod to Dr. Howl. She sees the two androids following him but there's no indication that she recognizes Lucy.

Dr. Howl nods back. He walks ahead of the Operator, leading the way.

There weren't any other scientists inside the lab the last time the Operator visited. This time, there's someone wearing a white lab coat at every workstation and surrounding the various industrial machines. Some scientists focus on the action inside their respective fume hoods, and others sit on stools in front of tables stacked high with small containers, pipetting small quantities of liquid while looking through protective goggles. With their focus on their various tasks, none notice the new arrivals.

Dr. Howl takes Lucy and the Operator to the last in a row of sealed rooms on the right side of the lab. The rest are all empty. The glass door slides open as Dr. Howl approaches, and he stands outside with his data pad in hand.

The Operator walks into the room according to Dr. Howl's clear intentions. He stands in the middle of the space with Lucy beside him. The walls are all white, and there's a rounded white bench on the back wall.

"Sit," Dr. Howl whispers.

In lockstep, the two androids step forward, turn around, and sit with their backs rigid and hands on their knees.

The glass door slides shut. "No one can hear us in here. Oh, almost forgot," Dr. Howl says. He punches some buttons on his data pad. "Had to turn the security guards back on," he says with a smile.

"But didn't they see us?" the Operator says, maintaining his posture.

"Wiped that bit from their memory," Dr. Howl says with a smile. With another series of taps on his data pad, the glass becomes opaque.

"You can relax," Dr. Howl says.

The Operator and Lucy take their hands from their knees but maintain their upright postures. "We need to get onto the seventy-fourth," the Operator says, his tone serious.

"Well, it's good to see you too!" Dr. Howl says, laughing. "I've been up here by myself, pretending to be the good scientist while feeding Pavlova information, and haven't talked to a single person who knows who I really am." Dr. Howl takes a big breath and exhales. "Feels good."

"Aren't you an android . . ." Lucy says, searching for an explanation.

"Oh, I'm not lonely! It feels good talking to someone else who's in on the joke."

"And nobody's suspected?" the Operator asks.

"Not a single one. Everyone listens without a second thought—you'd think all these humans are androids too! I brought in help since I don't know the first thing about running the city's science lab."

"I see that," the Operator says.

"Apparently, dealing with the real Dr. Howl was impossible. I just keep in mind that they're all humans; it's actually pretty easy."

The Operator nods. After a moment, he looks at Lucy, then back at Dr. Howl.

After a moment, Dr. Howl breaks the silence. "So, the seventy-fourth. I've been looking for a reason to give the resort a visit." He looks at Lucy. "Of course, an *android* couldn't possibly appreciate the amenities," he says with a smirk.

Lucy opens her mouth but Dr. Howl continues before she speaks.

"But I'm curious about what humans find so appealing."

"You're going up too?" the Operator asks.

"How do you think you're getting up there? You two are my escorts!"

The Operator raises his eyebrows. "And you can just walk onto that high of a level, no questions asked?"

"I'm the city's leading scientist—not just by reputation. My *lab* is on the forty-second, but I can go wherever I want." Dr. Howl gives the Operator a mischievous smile. "Nice little perk."

The Operator looks at Lucy. "Just one problem: What are we going to do about her face?"

Lucy looks at Dr. Howl with her head at a slight tilt. The Operator follows her gaze.

"What's wrong with her face? I think she's lovely."

Both the Operator and Lucy roll their eyes. "You know what I mean," the Operator says.

"The entire city is looking for me," Lucy adds.

"Do you think we should . . . replace it?"

"Take another face? We don't have to do all that. You two

can just wear some helmets. If the Enforcers can walk around with half of their faces obscured by their Hololenses, there's no reason you can't cover your faces. If anyone asks, I'll say it's new tech—threat detection or something like that."

Dr. Howl sees the Operator's disbelieving face and continues. "I'm telling you, nobody questions anything." He brings his data pad back up and punches a series of commands.

"Uniforms are ordered; should be here soon. The helmets are the ones used by the transport drivers. Nobody uses them now that no one flies, thanks to Jirasek." He looks up to the ceiling as he says the name, as if he's seeing straight through the building above to the ship hovering over the city.

Dr. Howl sits on the ground with his back to the clouded glass while they wait together for the uniforms' arrival. He asks questions about Pavlova, about Sigma, and has trouble believing the entire district attacked Chance. "What were they thinking?" he says after hearing the news.

Lucy, already silent for the most part, becomes downright sullen while the Operator recounts the battle. He doesn't mention her contribution to the victory, other than to discuss how she saved the bartender's life.

"She's lucky you were there," Dr. Howl says.

"Yeah, good thing," Lucy says in a faraway voice.

Someone knocks on the glass and Dr. Howl stands up. "They're here," he says with excitement. The Operator and Lucy both place their hands on their knees.

Dr. Howl pushes a button on his data pad and the glass slides open. Instead of a uniform delivery, a lone security android wearing dark gray compression stands outside.

"What?" Dr. Howl says, annoyed, when the android doesn't say a word.

"Yoshiko Apocalypse just arrived. She requires your assistance."

The Operator makes sure his face stays expressionless and hopes Lucy has the same thought.

"Please tell her I'll be right with her," Dr. Howl says.

The security android turns and walks towards the port.

"Well, this is a surprise. I'll leave the door open a crack for the delivery," Dr. Howl says before leaving the room.

The Operator and Lucy don't wait long. A scientist in a white lab coat brings a thick package and two helmets into the room, depositing them on the floor while speaking to the inert pair sitting on the white bench. "Dr. Howl said to leave these in here on the floor," they say while staring at the room's two occupants. The Operator waits for a flash of recognition when they see Lucy's face, but none emerges. The scientist backs out of the room and hurries away.

After waiting a moment, the Operator hurries forward and grabs the package. He rips it open and throws a dark gray compression suit to Lucy. "Put this on," he says.

Lucy waits until the last moment before raising her hand and catching the garment. She puts it on in a rush, leaving her clothes in a pile on the floor, following the Operator's lead. A pair of matching thin, dark gray shoes also came in the package—both the Operator and Lucy agree with a look that they'll continue using their black boots. The Operator wraps his holster around his waist while Lucy puts her blaster in the built-in pocket. They put the helmets on last.

"Should we just sit here and wait for him to get back?" Lucy says, her voice muffled.

The Operator shakes his head no. "Come on," he says. Walking tall, the Operator leads Lucy back through the lab and out into the port.

"It doesn't matter how it happened! I just need it fixed," Yoshiko screams. She's standing in the middle of the port with her exoskeleton at her feet and Hololenses on her head, at the foot of a set of stairs that lead down from one of the parked hovercrafts the Operator saw when he climbed into the port. Behind her are the four other members of her team, each still wearing their exoskeletons and Hololenses.

The Operator continues walking across the port, straight at Dr. Howl.

"Knowing how you damaged it will help us make effective repairs and improvements on the design," Dr. Howl says in an even tone. He crouches down and inspects the gunmetal skeleton sitting on the floor. "Appears you cracked one of the forearm supports," he says.

"And who are you?" Yoshiko says to the helmeted Operator and Lucy.

Dr. Howl stands up and brushes his hand against his black pants. "Security androids. Nothing to worry about, Ms. Apocalypse."

"You called security on me?" Yoshiko says, glaring at Dr. Howl.

"The elevated volume of your speaking triggered them," Dr. Howl says, unflinching. "I can send them back to the lab if they make you uncomfortable."

"No need. Maybe lower your trigger sensitivity, I'm not even mad," Yoshiko says, making an effort at keeping her voice at a conversational level.

"I'll look into it. You can leave the suit here, I'll have a mech take it over to the lab."

Yoshiko nods. She turns to her team and tells them they'll use the building's elevators before starting across the port.

"Still not going to tell me what did this to your suit?" Dr. Howl says as she walks past him.

Yoshiko exhales and releases her scrunched-up face. "I did it myself," she says, as if admitting it bothers her more than the damaged suit. "I punched some Sigma surface-dweller's garage door, didn't realize it was reinforced."

Dr. Howl waits.

"Found out the missing android and the guy protecting her were in Sigma and they got away."

CHAPTER EIGHTEEN

The Operator expects an elaborate series of walkways, back hallways, checkpoints, and staircases on their way up to the island resort on the seventy-fourth. Instead, he and Lucy follow Dr. Howl through two expansive, well-lit tunnels on their way to a third building; each has a checkpoint with a lone khaki-wearing guard standing watch who doesn't even ask the prominent scientist for identification. Then, they get into the largest elevator car he's ever seen. Every surface is reflective stainless steel.

Dr. Howl puts his face up to a hand-sized black screen with green lines. A small light in the corner turns from red to green. "Which floor?" a disembodied voice says from above.

"Seventy-four," Dr. Howl replies.

The elevator springs into action, gaining speed as it propels the group up towards their destination. Dr. Howl looks at Lucy and the Operator and gives them a slight smile and a head nod before turning away. The Operator wonders if the scientist saw a reflection of himself in the helmet's black visor.

Their speed decreases as they approach the target floor,

until they stop after a graceful final deceleration. The doors don't open right away.

The Operator's hand creeps down to his side, hovering over his blaster. If someone found out who they are and set up a trap . . .

"Welcome to paradise," the disembodied voice above says. Then, the doors slide apart, displaying a colorful, noisy reception area. The wall ahead is a live-action view of the ocean, waves lapping against a thin line of sand at the bottom of the screen. A row of smiling, attractive men and women, all bronzed and wearing bathing suits or bikinis, stands on each side of the elevator, with every race and size represented.

The ceremony wasn't a part of the Operator's first visit, the only other time he'd been to the island resort level. The week-long stay with his former betrothed was a memory he'd rather forget.

Dr. Howl leads the way through the welcome lines. The Operator and Lucy follow, walking next to each other in Dr. Howl's wake. The scientist looks off to one side and nods to an androgynous receptionist with blond hair, wearing a simple blue sport jacket behind a front desk. They nod back with a smile.

With a full view of the wall ahead, the Operator sees that people can walk to the left or right of the moving image. The left and right walls are also live-action shots of the sea, giving the impression of being on a small sand island surrounded by water on all sides. The last individuals in the welcome line—two on the right, one on the left—hold bright floral leis out, ready for the three visitors' heads. Dr. Howl accepts the first lei and gives an acquiescent nod, permitting the placement of the colorful wreaths over the heads of the helmeted Operator and Lucy.

With their helmets on, both androids nod down and accept the decoration.

When Dr. Howl turns and approaches the reception desk,

followed by his security detail, the welcome lines walk away from the elevator, further splitting as they go to each side of the screen depicting the ocean.

"Welcome to paradise," the receptionist says, repeating the elevator's message. "What can we do for you?"

"I'd like a room. Two nights should be enough for a quick recharge," Dr. Howl says.

"The trouble will be pulling yourself away from here when it's time to go back," the receptionist says with a smile. They pull a data pad from the desk and punch a series of numbers. "We already have your account—" they say. Then, noticing Dr. Howl's inquisitive look, they add, "From the elevator."

"Of course, of course. My security detail shouldn't be a problem, correct?"

"Not at all. Many of our guests feel safer with their own precautions in place, despite our close relationship with the city's top Enforcers. I trust you want them staying with you?"

"Yes." After a moment, Dr. Howl asks where else they would stay.

"We have a temporary barracks for security personnel that they are welcome to use."

"Oh, that won't be necessary."

The receptionist finishes typing on the data pad. "You're all set. Room four seventeen. It'll open with your facial scan."

Dr. Howl taps the desk twice. The Operator remembers that the skinless android who took over Dr. Howl's life was a concierge for Pavlova, and he wonders if the android picked up the tapping gesture from an important client or Pavlova himself.

"Wait, it's your first time here, isn't it?" the receptionist says. She taps her data pad a number of times, confirming the answer to her question before Dr. Howl can respond. "Yes. So there are four main halls going away from the main resort area—one on the left, three on the right. Your room is the seventeenth one in the fourth hall," she says, her arm held out behind her and to the right.

Dr. Howl leads the Operator and Lucy to the right of the wall blocking the view of the island resort from the elevator. There's a short overlap area before they emerge into paradise.

The three of them stand on a wooden walkway that extends far into the distance on both sides. There's a door close by for the welcome party. The seventy-fourth level of the city is famous for taking up a large swath of real estate, extending past typical building borders. Instead of tunnels connecting the buildings on this level, there are vertical tunnels built into the layout for hovercrafts traveling between levels, unused now that Jirasek stopped all air traffic.

The resort doesn't take up the entire city's seventy-fourth level—on the far corner is a checkpoint where an incoming horizontal tunnel meets the establishment. Seeing the checkpoint in the distance, the Operator turns around and looks in the opposite direction, finding another.

Lucy doesn't pay attention to the corners; she's facing the resort itself. Ahead of her is the deep end of a massive wave pool, with arched wooden bridges extending over it at every block that lead to the sandy beach in the distance. On the beach are people lounging in spaced-out cabanas, sitting under umbrellas, and lying on towels in open areas of sand. Behind the sand are restaurants and stores with wooden plank exteriors, thatched roofs, and hanging surfboards and life preservers. A large numbered plaque hangs above each hallway's entrance.

Artificial sunlight shines down on it all from an artificial blue sky overhead.

The memory of Patrice lying on a towel, drinking from a straw in a coconut with sand in her hair, strikes the Operator before he can suppress the recollection. He closes his eyes, shakes his head, and refocuses on Dr. Howl, falling into his role as android security for protection from his own thoughts.

Dr. Howl leads the way over the closest wooden bridge. A few curious beachgoers watch them, inspecting the helmet-wearing Operator and Lucy, but so many visitors have security stationed around them that those looking soon lose interest. They walk along the boardwalk at the end of the bridge through the beach, then turn and follow the walkway along the front of the shops. The Operator makes a special effort of not paying attention to the various shops and patrons, his eyes forward at all times, hoping nothing else triggers a memory.

Their assigned room is a large suite with a sitting area and two bedrooms—a master bedroom and another, smaller room with two small beds. A balcony attached to the sitting room has a screen that replicates an oceanfront view, complete with dunes and beach grasses swaying in the breeze.

The Operator and Lucy take off their helmets right away, depositing their leis on a chair next to Dr. Howl's discarded adornment. Lucy runs a hand through her hair, tousling it and swiping it to one side.

"We should start looking for our hacker," Dr. Howl says, sitting down on a couch in the sitting area and holding his data pad in front of him. He turns it around. "Pavlova sent me his name and a picture of his face."

On the data pad screen is a thick-necked young man with a square jaw, symmetrical face, and striking eyes.

"*That's* the hacker?" Lucy says in disbelief.

"That's the picture Pavlova gave me. Hold on." Dr. Howl turns the data pad back to himself and punches some more buttons. "Yes, it says he's here. Jacinto Caballero, staying in room three twenty-four."

"You can see that information?" the Operator says. Part of him wonders if Dr. Howl can also see the archived records, and the archived footage—if evidence of his presence in the island resort still exists anywhere besides his memory.

"City's top scientist," Dr. Howl says, tapping his temple. "Let's go see if we can find him. He should be out and about—no way he traveled all the way up here just to sit in his room."

Dr. Howl leans back and puts his hands on his knees before using his forward momentum to stand up. He pauses when he sees Lucy staring at him.

"We're going to go out there like this?" she says, gesturing towards her suit. Then, she points at Dr. Howl's work attire.

"Sure. We've just arrived, out getting some food. We can start over in front of hall three—I doubt he'd go very far from there."

Lucy mutters something under her breath that the Operator doesn't hear.

"What was that?" Dr. Howl says.

"I'm tired of the helmet," Lucy says, exasperated but resigned.

"It's your face that got plastered all over the city," Dr. Howl reminds her. "If anyone's complaining, it should be him," he says, pointing to the Operator.

The Operator puts his helmet on, looks at Lucy through the black visor, and shrugs. "Could be worse," he says, his words muffled.

Lucy gives him a glare before putting on her own helmet. Then, they follow Dr. Howl back down the fourth hallway, along the walkway in front of the shop, and stand in front of hallway three.

"What now?" Lucy asks, standing next to the Operator while they look around.

The Operator shrugs. He takes a look at a tanned, wrinkled woman in a thin, bright blue bikini walking by, her skin providing clear evidence of years of sun exposure. Her face has a thin sheen of sweat and oil, reminding the Operator about how hot the beach was the last time he was there. He remembers sweating on a towel in the sand, but before his memory can devolve further he thinks about the compression suit he wears and admires its cooling capability. His head is hot in the helmet, but with his body comfortable, it's tolerable.

"Let's go sit down," Dr. Howl says, approaching a restaurant at the corner of the boardwalk and hallway three.

Lucy follows right behind Dr. Howl, with the Operator bringing up the rear. He pretends he's scoping for threats while in truth, he's looking for the hacker. He doesn't find him.

To the surprise of the hostess, Dr. Howl insists on a table near the foot traffic. She tries putting him closer to the restaurant's interior twice, with each table vetoed by Dr. Howl, before letting the scientist choose his own seat. He picks the one farthest from the restaurant's center, protected from the boardwalk by a thick knotted rope hanging from moveable wooden posts.

"Perfect," Dr. Howl says, taking a seat. The hostess hands out menus and says, "The waiter will be with you shortly."

When Dr. Howl sees the Operator and Lucy still standing, he insists that they sit down too. "Can't take off the helmets, but you can at least rest your feet."

Together, the three of them scan the island resort, searching for the hacker's face. While none of the spaces in the island resort seem crowded at first glance, the sheer size allows for an impressive number of people. All types walk past, and more stay in place on the beach. "Think he's somewhere out there?" Dr. Howl asks after glasses of water arrive.

"Could be. He has to go back to his room sometime though."

"Then, we wait."

The Operator watches a thin young man with long arms and thin legs approach a number of women lying on the beach, both exposed to the sun and beneath umbrellas. He chuckles to himself as the young Casanova tries a series of strategies for getting the women's attention, his expressions and body language ranging from goofy to serious. Over time, the young man works his way towards where the Operator, Dr. Howl, and Lucy sit, turning around and looking for a woman or women he hasn't tried approaching. Finding none, he turns around and walks into the restaurant.

Inspired, the Operator leans across the table, closer to Dr. Howl. "Can you see where the hacker spends his money?" he whispers.

"Only if he wants me to. Guy this good could probably just use a secret account."

Dr. Howl pokes at his data pad, then looks at the Operator in surprise before turning and looking inside of the restaurant. "He just—"

"Shhh," the Operator says as the young man passes behind him with a drink in hand.

"Jacinto changed his official identification picture," Dr. Howl mutters, suppressing a laugh.

The hacker walks down hallway three with the three androids following behind. He stops once on the way to his room because of a coughing fit after taking a drink, and he's still fighting back coughs when he gets to his room and puts his face to the scanner.

The reflection of the two looming helmets in the darkened screen makes him turn around as the light in the corner switches from red to green and the door unlocks.

CHAPTER NINETEEN

"Sit," Dr. Howl says, pointing to the chair near the balcony's sliding glass door. Instead of a beach, the surrounding landscape is the inside of a classic Western brothel—women wearing scarlet dresses with black lace sitting on men's laps, the men all wearing cowboy hats and bandanas around their necks. Seen up close, the hacker is a young man, little more than a teen, with tan skin, tousled black hair, and the beginnings of a thin mustache. His face gets red when he sees Dr. Howl noticing the scene outside his window, and he reaches behind him and closes the blinds.

"Didn't like the standard view?" Dr. Howl asks.

Jacinto shrugs. "Not hard to change," he says.

The hacker's room is bigger than the one given to Dr. Howl. It has three bedrooms and a large table that seats eight behind where the hacker sits facing the fireplace on the right wall. The Operator and Lucy walk around the couch and sit down facing the balcony, and Dr. Howl sits in another chair facing the fireplace, a small table separating his chair from Jacinto's.

"So, what do you want?" Jacinto says, contempt coloring his voice.

"We need you to hack into Jirasek's network," the Operator says before Dr. Howl can speak.

The scientist glares at the Operator. "Well, now that our cards are on the table . . ." he says.

Jacinto crosses his arms. "Why would I help you?"

Dr. Howl turns back towards Jacinto and leans in his direction, his elbow resting on the chair's arm. "Look, we're sorry about the intrusion. We've heard about your abilities and were hoping we could come to some sort of . . . agreement."

"I'm listening."

"Well, it's obvious money isn't a problem for you," Dr. Howl says, looking around at the expansive room. "What do you want?"

"I can buy whatever I want," the hacker retorts, disgust written all over his face.

Dr. Howl nods. "Do you know who I am?" he asks.

"No idea," the hacker says, shaking his head. "Should I?"

"The city's top scientist. My lab developed and made Yoshiko's exoskeleton. I could get you one . . ."

"And what would I do with that? I don't really care about jumping between buildings, even if Jirasek didn't shoot down anything flying in the city."

The Operator stands up, takes off his helmet, withdraws his blaster, and aims it at Jacinto. "Well, do you care about staying alive?"

Dr. Howl takes a big breath and exhales as he leans back in his chair. "You'll have to forgive my friend." He extends an arm and waves his hand, telling the Operator to sit back down without words. "He gets a little . . . overeager."

The Operator sits back down but doesn't holster his blaster. Lucy takes off her helmet and Jacinto blushes.

Dr. Howl notices the hacker's response. "You know, my lab

can make an android that looks just like her—or anyone, for that matter. I *could* have one sent up, just for you."

"They're a headache; all the paperwork and registration."

"Unregistered. Nobody would know."

"*I* could tell," Jacinto says, his youthful self-assuredness shining through.

"Could you tell he was?" Dr. Howl says, pointing at the Operator.

Jacinto's eyes widen. "Really? Do they all have anger problems?"

"He's a special breed," Dr. Howl says, laughing.

Jacinto takes a quick glance at Lucy before his eyes drop to the left. Wrinkles form on his forehead. Then, in a flash, he lifts his head and looks at her again, this time unflinching. "I've seen you before," he whispers.

"The whole city has," Dr. Howl responds.

Jacinto's eyes get wide. "No wonder you want to go after Jirasek. He sent the whole city after you!"

"And we're going to make him pay," Lucy says, nodding.

"Well, this is probably the safest place for you," Jacinto says, leaning back in his chair and crossing his legs.

"Your room?" the Operator says, his words dripping with acidity.

"*No.* The upper levels. Specifically, this high and above."

"Ah," Dr. Howl says, lifting his chin. "Jirasek's reward means nothing to everyone already here."

"That, and everyone here can't stand how he's ground the city to a halt. They're all pissed: businessmen, politicians . . ."

"What about people who work for Jirasek? Don't they come here too?"

"Not anymore. They were blacklisted—the long-term guests wouldn't tolerate seeing them at the same restaurants and stores."

"How'd they know who works for Jirasek?" Lucy asks.

"Word gets out. I might have helped expose who funds their accounts . . ." Jacinto says with a sly grin.

"So you've already helped out the cause!" Dr. Howl says. "Why not take a swipe at Jirasek directly?"

"I never said I wouldn't; I just want to know what's in it for me. The world doesn't run on good intentions."

"Agreed," Dr. Howl says. He gives the Operator a stern glance, and the Operator presses his lips together. "You aren't interested in a high-end android? She'd be all yours."

Lucy looks away, disgusted.

"No . . . I'm interested in the real thing," Jacinto says.

"From the looks of things, I'd say they aren't interested in you," the Operator says with a chuckle.

Jacinto's cheeks and ears turn bright red. "What do you know? You're not even human," he snarls.

The Operator shakes his head. Lucy puts a hand on his leg, silencing him before he can answer.

"What if we helped you?" Lucy says.

"Help me what?" Jacinto says, his suspicious eyes focusing on Lucy. "Help the women here! They're the ones who don't appreciate the chance I'm giving them!"

Dr. Howl crosses his hands. "Doesn't take a human to recognize that mindset is what's keeping you alone at night."

Jacinto releases an exhale. "I don't really think like that; I just got mad."

"How we are when we lose control offers a glimpse at the truth," Dr. Howl says, sounding like a patient father explaining something to a frustrated son. He looks at the Operator, who's staring at him in surprise. "Something Zhang says when one of his experiments doesn't work. Surprisingly applicable."

Lucy leans forward, rests her elbows on her knees, and

interlocks her fingers. "Will you help us if we get you a date?" she asks.

Jacinto Caballero looks at her, blinks twice, and nods.

Dr. Howl leaves in search of clothes more suitable to the island resort's atmosphere. While he's gone, the Operator and Lucy talk to Jacinto about approaching women he's interested in.

"Now, the first thing to remember—" the Operator starts.

"Why would I listen to you? You're an *android*. What do you know about human women?"

The Operator looks at Lucy and she gives him a patient smile. He takes a deep breath. "You're right, I don't know anything." He stands up, walks behind the couch, and starts pacing so he doesn't say anything he'll regret. Patrice's memory pushes against the back of his skull while he keeps his thoughts focused on the room he's in and the people with him.

"The first thing to remember," Lucy says, picking up where the Operator left off. "Is that women are also people. People want friends."

"I don't want any friends."

"You want female friends, don't you?" Lucy asks, the tone of her voice sweeter than the Operator's ever heard.

"Well, yes," Jacinto admits.

"Okay then. And there are women who want male friends who don't know the first thing about talking to them, just like you. And women who want female friends, and men who want male friends . . ."

Jacinto's mouth slackens and hangs open as his eyes widen when the realization sinks in. "So, if I figure this out, I'm *helping* them make friends?"

Lucy laughs. "I've never thought about it like that; but, in a way, yes."

"So, let's say I see someone I'm interested in . . . being friends with. What do I say?"

"Just get them talking about themselves."

"Everyone's favorite topic," the Operator says from behind Lucy.

"Exactly."

"But what do I say *first*?"

"You just make conversation! For example, I noticed you have a Western background playing outside your balcony."

Jacinto nods. He seems less embarrassed about it than when they first walked in. "I used to watch old Western movies with my dad. I always thought they were cool."

Lucy gives Jacinto a kind smile.

"I just talked about myself," Jacinto says, laughing. "That's like a superpower!"

"If they're not interested in you, they'll just agree with you, or say nothing. But once they start sharing information all you have to do is keep the conversation flowing. For example, I could talk about movies I like, or something about Westerns I know."

"And when do I transition it to a date?"

"Oh okay, so once the conversation goes on for a while, just mention how you're going to get something to eat, either later or right then. Invite them."

"Everyone's gotta eat," the Operator adds.

Lucy nods.

"That's what I was doing wrong," Jacinto says, thinking. "I'd walk up to them and offer dinner right away, paid for by me."

"All you'll get with that approach is people who want free meals," says the Operator.

"Which is what happened," Jacinto replies. He doesn't hide his awe. "This is much more complicated than a computer," he adds, his voice trailing off.

Dr. Howl returns wearing khaki shorts, a blue Hawaiian

shirt, and sandals. He's carrying two bags, one with his old clothes; he hands the other to the Operator. Inside is a black swimsuit, a short-sleeved white button-down shirt with a black floral pattern, a dark blue sundress, and two pairs of white sneakers.

"I had to guess on the sizes," Dr. Howl says. He stays with Jacinto while the Operator and Lucy change into their outfits.

"You look like whole new people!" Dr. Howl says with pride when they emerge from their respective bedrooms. "Shoes fit all right?"

"Fine," Lucy says.

"A bit big," replies the Operator. His blaster sits against his lower back, tucked into the waistband.

"Oh well, close enough," says Dr. Howl. "Oh yeah, I almost forgot! These are for you." He pulls a pair of sunglasses with large circular lenses from his shirt pocket and hands them to Lucy. "I know he said nobody cares, but we can still take precautions."

Jacinto stands up and starts walking out. "Where do you think you're going?" the Operator says, standing in his way.

"To try and make some friends," he says with an appreciative glance at Lucy.

"We're coming with you."

Jacinto rolls his eyes. "Oh, this is going to work well. Hello, these are my escorts. They want me to take down Felipe Jirasek and won't leave me alone. Want to grab a bite to eat?"

Lucy puts a hand on the Operator's shoulder. "We'll stand back at the shops; you can go down to the beach and work your magic," she says with a wink.

"And I'll be at the beach if anyone needs me," Dr. Howl adds. The Operator grabs the bag with their clothes, his holster, and Lucy's blaster and together the four of them make their way down hallway three, back to the beach. Dr. Howl turns towards hallway four, saying he'll "do his own thing." Jacinto walks onto the sand in front of hallway three while the Operator and Lucy stand on the boardwalk, near a taco restaurant.

Jacinto walks up to three different women before he sits down with one while they talk. He gestures back towards the boardwalk, at the restaurant near his overwatch. Then, to the Operator's surprise, a young woman packs up her bag and walks with him back to their location.

"Hey guys!" Jacinto says, walking straight up to Lucy and the Operator. He turns to his new friend. "These are my friends I told you I was meeting. Guys, this is Claire."

"Nice to meet you," Lucy says with a smile and a slight bow.

"Pleasure," the Operator grunts.

"Should we head in?" Jacinto says. He ushers the three of them inside and they get seated at a table near the back.

Lucy takes off her sunglasses when she sits down and sets them on the table.

"So, Claire, how long are you staying on the seventy-fourth?"

Claire rearranges her bikini bottom before settling back down. "Just for two weeks." She looks at Jacinto. "Actually, could you order me a water? I need to use the restroom."

Jacinto smiles. "Of course."

The Operator leans in and hisses at Jacinto when Claire leaves. "What were you thinking? A date with us?"

"Sorry! I froze. I was worried I'd run out of things to say." He looks at Lucy. "She makes it look so easy."

Lucy smiles. "They're all humans."

"And now she's seen her face. Up close," the Operator says.

"Relax, he said nobody here cares," Lucy says, picking up the menu.

"Nobody here *long-term* cares. She's just here on vacation. Maybe she wants to become one of the long-term visitors!"

"You're just being paranoid."

The Operator stands up, and before Jacinto or Lucy can stop him, walks towards the restroom. On his way there, he glances into the kitchen and sees a nervous Claire with a phone held up to her ear. He storms through the double doors and snatches it from her hand.

Claire yells one final message before the Operator ends the call: "They know you're coming! Hurry!"

CHAPTER TWENTY

"Who'd you call?" the Operator says, suppressing his rage.

Claire looks at him with defiance written on her face.

"Who'd you call!" the Operator roars.

"My aunt," a startled Claire says.

"You're lying," the Operator seethes.

Claire shakes her head. "She . . . she works for the Enforcers below the fiftieth."

Lucy and Jacinto come running to the kitchen, alerted after hearing the Operator yell.

"What's going on?" Lucy says. She looks at the phone and at the terrified Claire. "Who'd she call?"

"Enforcers."

"So?" Jacinto says, approaching Claire.

The Operator grabs Jacinto's arm. "We've got to go."

Jacinto tries pulling away but it's no use.

"Where's the bag?" the Operator asks Lucy.

"At the table."

"Come on."

The three of them—Jacinto dragged along—go back to the table and retrieve the bag. The Operator and Lucy change back into the dark gray compression suits Dr. Howl provided for them right next to the table, disregarding the onlookers. While tying their boots, Lucy asks the Operator if they should go back to Jacinto's room and get their helmets.

"Don't see why. There's no point in hiding your face anymore—they already know you're here."

"Good point. What about Howl?"

The Operator thinks for a moment. "Let's go find him."

They run towards the fourth hallway then turn onto the beach, surveying every direction for the incoming Enforcers. After running past dozens of relaxing beachgoers in the sand, they find the scientist with his eyes closed on a dark wooden chair beneath a bright red umbrella.

Dr. Howl opens his eyes without moving his head. He sits up when he sees their uniforms. "What's going on?"

"Enforcers are on their way."

Dr. Howl takes a quick look behind him, then along the water's edge in both directions. "What the hell were you thinking coming to me!" he says. "I can't be seen with you—they'll know I helped you!" He stands up from his chair and starts running towards the fourth hall. The trio follow. "If they even find out I'm up here at the same time as you it looks suspicious! And when they see you wearing those uniforms . . ." Dr. Howl shakes his head in despair.

They get onto the boardwalk. "Get away from here," Dr. Howl says. "I'll go back to my room and get back to the lab as soon as I can. So much for my little vacation."

The Operator turns to Jacinto while Dr. Howl retreats into the distance. "Do you know which way Jirasek Tower is?"

Jacinto points to the corner across the water past hallway one.

"Let's go."

They start running along the boardwalk, past gawking vacationers. Jacinto stops as they pass hallway three. "I'm not risking my neck for you two," he says.

"The hell you're not," the Operator says, grabbing the young man.

Jacinto tries pulling away without success. The mother of a nearby family in a restaurant notices and yells, "Let him go!" Then, turning to her husband, she says, "Do something!"

The husband takes one look at the Operator and shrugs. His wife hits his upper arm with the back of her hand.

Lucy steps forward, breaking the Operator's hold on Jacinto with her body. She grabs the hacker's shoulders with her hands and shakes him. "We had a deal, right?"

Jacinto looks down the third hall.

"Look at me!" Lucy urges. Jacinto focuses on her face. "We had a deal, didn't we?"

"I didn't know we would be running from Enforcers!"

"But we had a deal! You got a date, now you help us."

"The date got cut short!"

"But you got one, didn't you? That was the deal. And now you know how to get more, right?"

Jacinto nods.

"Okay then. Now it's time for you to hold up your end of the bargain."

"But *Enforcers?*"

"Not just any Enforcer—Yoshiko," the Operator says.

The Operator points at the bridge leading from the elevator entrance to the beach. There, running across, is Yoshiko Apocalypse and her team, all wearing their trademark black Hololenses. Her four supporting members wear their exoskeletons; Yoshiko runs without hers. She's still wearing her black tights and black tank top, the tattoo sleeves on both arms on full display.

"Come on," the Operator says, running ahead. Lucy puts a

hand on Jacinto's lower back; the hacker sighs and starts running as well, with Lucy bringing up the rear. They make it to the second hall before seeing Yoshiko and her team blocking the path ahead of them.

The Operator crouches behind a concrete planter and fires at the group through leaves. His shot hits one member of the unprepared Enforcer team in the chest and they drop. The rest of the squadron takes cover—Yoshiko and one member in a shop on the right side of the boardwalk, the other two behind a cabana on the beach.

The vacationers in the area start screaming and running away from the confrontation, blocking the path between the Operator and Yoshiko's position. In the commotion, a gloved hand from behind the cabana reaches out and drags the fallen Enforcer onto the beach.

"That you, Lucy?" Yoshiko calls out when there's no one left in the area but the two groups.

The Operator looks at Lucy where she's hiding with Jacinto behind another planter. Jacinto's head is between his knees, his hands over his ears. "She's here," he yells. He shrugs, and tells Lucy there's no point in hiding it.

"And you must be the one she's been running around with."

The Operator sees Yoshiko peek out from behind the store's wall in the distance. He fires a shot, but she pulls away a moment before, anticipating the action.

"Tell her to come with us—you can just walk away."

"Afraid I can't do that," the Operator replies.

The artificial beach breezes blow the towels left behind on chairs, the waves lap at the shore, and hanging wind chimes deliver soft tones into the air.

Two Enforcers emerge from behind the row of cabanas, on the Operator's left, aiming in his general direction. It's clear they don't know his exact hiding place, and he takes aim before they discover him. The moving foliage gives away his position and the Enforcers spin away as he shoots, back behind cover. His last shot ricochets off the gunmetal brace on one of their arms.

With the bulk of the Operator's attention on the two beach-side Enforcers, the Enforcer on Yoshiko's side wearing an exoskeleton walks out of the store and jumps straight up in the air. The Operator sees the flash just after he shoots at the retreating beachside Enforcers, and he aims his blaster at the ceiling above Yoshiko. It's too late for an effective shot—the Enforcer disappears behind a hidden ledge where the artificial sky meets the storefront.

"Now would be a good time to get out that blaster," the Operator says to Lucy.

She shakes her head.

"We have you surrounded," Yoshiko calls out.

"Look, you don't have to go into a trance. Just help out. I can't take care of all three sides." A rustling overhead pulls the Operator's attention towards the ceiling, and he fires a warning shot into the space. Without waiting for a reason, he fires another two shots at the edge of the cabana, kicking up sand.

Lucy pulls her blaster out and takes a series of deep breaths. "Stay with me," the Operator says. "Just like when we were in the alley. Target practice."

"Target practice," Lucy repeats. Jacinto picks his head up, looks at the Operator and Lucy, then returns to his cowering.

"Just take care of overhead."

Lucy turns around and aims above, while the Operator handles the beachside Enforcers and Yoshiko on the boardwalk. The lead Enforcer doesn't expose herself often and has minimal movement capabilities compared to the two behind the cabana, so the Operator focuses most of his attention on making sure they don't flank him. The standoff drags on, with Lucy firing a handful of shots overhead, until the two Enforcers on the beach disappear for too long. Then, one shows up on either side of the cabana, shooting at the Operator with their comrade and pinning him down.

The shots from the Enforcer closest to the Operator on the beach get closer, but there's nothing he can do. He looks past the edge of the concrete planter, waiting for the first body part he can shoot . . .

"Fall back!" Yoshiko calls out.

The blaster fire stops. Heavy footfalls overhead retreat into the distance, towards Yoshiko.

Lucy, Jacinto, and the Operator peer over the concrete planters. Yoshiko directs one Enforcer from the beach up into the artificial sky, and the other drags their fallen comrade into the shop with her. Then, farther in the distance and coming from the corner leading to Jirasek Tower, a group of metal androids runs up the beach from where they landed after flying over the water.

Jirasek's androids, the same model as the ones from Gamma's market—gleaming silver, flamethrowers attached to their left arms, blasters on their right. And, the Operator now knows, thrusters in their boots.

"Who are they?" Jacinto asks, awestruck.

"Jirasek's," the Operator responds.

"This just keeps getting better," Jacinto says, shaking his head.

Jirasek's androids take up position near the first hallway and start shooting at the Enforcers. Yoshiko keeps poking her head out and looking at the Operator and Lucy's position.

"Get ready," the Operator whispers. He waits until the next time Yoshiko looks and pulls her head back, then tells the other two, "Now!"

They run across the boardwalk to the cabanas on the beach,

crouching behind them and moving forward with the sound of blaster fire and crashing waves surrounding them.

The Operator gestures to the bridge crossing over the water. "Keep your heads down," he says.

"We're running into the open? Are you crazy!" Jacinto hisses.

"Have any other ideas?" the Operator asks—a genuine question.

Jacinto shakes his head and lowers his gaze. "All for a date," he mutters.

Lucy tucks her blaster into the holster at her side. "A deal's a deal."

The Operator peers around the edge of the cabana, making sure both Jirasek's androids and the Enforcers are preoccupied. As he watches, one of Jirasek's androids flies up to the ceiling, going after the two Enforcers raining fire down on them from overhead. The android drops back down soon after with a gaping hole in its chest.

"Let's go," the Operator says. The three of them run over the beach and make it to the bridge. The Operator stops at the bridge's entrance and makes sure Lucy and Jacinto cross before he does. At the shop, he sees Yoshiko look at him—now wearing her fallen comrade's exoskeleton—with surprise written all over her face. She starts walking forward, but blaster fire reminds her of Jirasek's androids and she steps back into the shop.

The shots directed at them begin when Lucy, Jacinto, and the Operator are at the bridge's apex. Jirasek's androids, noticing the fleeing trio, start directing their fire at the group. Yoshiko's Enforcers make the ones who forget about them pay, hitting the silver androids with blaster fire that knocks them to the ground. Somehow, the Operator and his group make it to the long wooden walkway running along the back side of the massive wave pool unharmed. They turn right and run towards Jirasek

Tower, passing the reception area outside the elevator. It's abandoned, with multicolored floral leis on the ground and no sign of where the employees went.

"Wait!" the Operator commands before Lucy runs out from behind the wall depicting the ocean that separates the reception area from the island resort. Jacinto stops when she does. The Operator moves forward and peeks at the scene across the water. Yoshiko and the Enforcer in the shop with her stare in his direction as two of Jirasek's androids take flight using their boot thrusters.

"Don't let them—!" Yoshiko yells, pointing at the flying androids.

The two Enforcers overhead launch themselves horizontal and intercept the androids before they get far. They withdraw their shotguns from their back holsters when they hit the ground and fire into the writhing androids, who collapse. The remaining androids focus their fire on the two exposed Enforcers, who jump high in the air and execute a backflip before landing on a cabana, collapsing through the ceiling.

Yoshiko points at Jirasek's androids and the Enforcer with her starts laying cover fire. Then, Yoshiko runs forward, clearing the space between herself and the androids with powerful bounds. With her shotgun, she shoots the first three she encounters. The next two try taking off to the far side of the water, but Yoshiko grabs both of their feet and holds on, digging her heels into the sand and twisting her face away from the thrusters' flames.

The Operator realizes he won't have a better chance—he grabs both Jacinto and Lucy, pulling them forward before letting go and running as fast as he can.

CHAPTER TWENTY-ONE

THE SOUND of blaster fire follows the Operator, Jacinto, and Lucy down the expansive tunnel between the island resort and Jirasek Tower. Thin carpet muffles their footfalls as they run. Their destination looms ahead, one of the tallest buildings in the city, looking down on the fleeing trio through the tunnel's glass walls. Through the right wall, the Operator sees Jirasek's ship hovering over the city. Lucy follows the Operator's gaze then turns back to him, flexes her jaw, and nods once.

A lone silver android up ahead sits inert in front of a computer at a desk on the right side of the tunnel. A nylon strap built into the left wall ends at a metal stand near the desk, leaving space for a single person to pass through to the building beyond. As the group approaches, the android wakes up with a jerk, as if a marionette pulls on strings from above. Their arms, hanging limp at their side moments before, rise up to the desk and rest near the keyboard.

"Identification," they say in a pleasant voice.

The Operator pulls out his blaster and shoots the android between their eyes. Their head falls forward, hitting the keyboard's keys.

"Shouldn't have done that," Jacinto says, pulling a thin data pad and a cord from his pocket.

All of a sudden, a wailing alarm rings out, accompanied by flashing lights emerging from the ceiling.

While the Operator and Lucy watch motionless, Jacinto runs around the desk and plugs into the computer. "I can get into the building's security, but the main network runs through the control room," he says. After a series of rapid keystrokes, he looks at the Operator with eyes full of mock disappointment, then shakes his head. The lights retract back into the ceiling, and the alarm stops.

An eerie silence descends on their end of the tunnel, punctuated by the occasional blaster going off in the distance.

"We don't have time for this," the Operator says, looking back and expecting Yoshiko Apocalypse at any moment.

"We do if you don't want the reinforcements sent for us arriving before we get to that control room," Jacinto counters. A few more strokes and he unplugs from the computer. "I looped this android's past two minutes indefinitely—they'll never knows he's off-line." He taps the silver android's shoulder, then looks at an unknown fluid on his hand.

"Wait, plug back in," the Operator tells Jacinto while the hacker wipes his hand on his pants.

"Why?" Jacinto says while following instructions.

"Send a group of androids here, in case the Enforcers follow."

"Good idea," Lucy says, turning around and looking, along with the Operator, at where the tunnel meets the island resort.

They don't wait long—Jacinto reports the android security is on their way seconds later. "They'll have quite the welcome party," Jacinto says, putting the data pad and cord back into his pocket.

They start running deeper into the building. The walls are

dark brown, with yellow light from artificial torches on intermittent sconces adding to the illumination from fluorescent overhead lights.

"Which way?" Lucy asks.

"I downloaded a map," Jacinto says, tapping his pocket. "Keep going this way for now."

They continue down the hall and turn right, following Jacinto's instructions, where they come face-to-face with a mass of jogging androids. Three across and ten deep, the androids show no signs of stopping when they see the intruders.

The Operator pins himself against one wall, Lucy and Jacinto against the other.

"I made the tunnel their primary priority," Jacinto yells over the sound of the android traffic. "They won't pay any attention to us."

They step away from the walls once the androids pass and reconvene in the center, Jacinto with a wide grin on his face. "Let's see the Enforcers get past *that*." The hacker pulls out his data pad and consults the map. "There should be a staircase up ahead on the right. We can take that up to the ninety-ninth, then cut through the cafeteria to the stairs that take us to the control room on the hundredth."

"Lead the way," Lucy says.

Jacinto starts off jogging but slows to a walk when they get to the stairs. His breathing becomes labored while they climb, and he pulls himself forward with his arms using the handrails. At one point, the Operator puts a hand on his lower back and forces his continued movement.

"Maybe I should exercise more," Jacinto says while resting his hands on his knees when they get to the ninety-ninth floor. He stands up, puts his arms over his head, and gulps air with his eyes closed.

When his eyes open again, he sees the Operator and Lucy

staring at him—Lucy with kind humor, and the Operator in anger.

"You done?" the Operator says.

Jacinto takes two more deep breaths. "Done." He pulls out his data pad and looks at the map before putting it away. "Let's go."

The three of them walk out into an opulent hall of offices, with thick blue carpet and clean white walls. Each door along the hall has a plaque installed next to it, and the doors are rich dark wood with frosted glass windows.

"Act like we belong here," the Operator says.

They walk towards the cafeteria, the Operator in front, Lucy behind him, and Jacinto bringing up the rear.

"I don't think anyone's in these," Jacinto says from behind when they're halfway down the hall.

The Operator turns around and finds the hacker with his face against one of the windows with his hands against his temples. He rushes forward and rips Jacinto away from the door. "How is that acting like we belong here?" he snarls.

"Listen," Jacinto says, becoming quiet. The Operator realizes the intense silence and looks at Lucy. She shrugs.

"This place is deserted," Jacinto whispers.

"Maybe they're all in the cafeteria. On their lunch break."

"Still seems too quiet."

The Operator watches as Lucy walks to the closest office and reaches for the handle.

"Wait," the Operator hisses.

Lucy looks at him and pushes the handle down. It's unlocked. The door rests ajar for a moment before Lucy pushes it further.

The office is spotless. There are organized folders and books on the bookcase, and a nameplate on the desk that matches the plaque outside the door, but no signs of recent usage.

Before the Operator can stop her, Lucy opens another office. Then another, while he watches. Each one has evidence of assignment but no recent occupation.

"This doesn't make sense. Where is everyone?" Lucy asks. She opens another door and comes face-to-face with someone standing stock-still in the center of the room, facing the other direction. Their head turns with a sudden abruptness, followed by their body, and they start marching towards Lucy with stiff, mechanical steps.

"It's an android," Jacinto whispers.

The Operator withdraws his blaster while Lucy slams the door shut.

"Don't just leave it in there! What if it activates the alarm again!" the Operator says.

"Doubt that old thing even knows what an alarm is," Jacinto says with a smirk.

The Operator lets go of Jacinto and approaches the door just as it opens. He raises his blaster and shoots the android right between the eyes, sending wires and sparks flying through the back of its head.

Jacinto rushes into the room and plugs his data pad into the computer on the desk.

"There's no record of an android in this room," he says. "Must be a personal model." He continues typing on his data pad. Then, he looks at the Operator and Lucy in alarm. "There's no humans on this level because they're all on the ship."

"Voluntarily?"

"Doesn't say, but I doubt it."

"We're the only humans up here," Jacinto says, looking at Lucy. "If any of the androids see us up here—" He looks at the Operator. "You're fine."

"Well, he looks like a human too. They wouldn't be able to tell at first glance."

"Can't you take off your skin or something?"

"Not that easy—" the Operator begins.

"Too many fluids," Lucy finishes.

"You work with androids before this one?" Jacinto says to Lucy, nodding towards the Operator.

"Something like that," Lucy says, exchanging a knowing smile with the Operator.

"What?" Jacinto snaps, in a flash of stubborn juvenile curiosity at being left out of the joke.

Lucy looks at Jacinto. "I'm an android too."

Jacinto sets the data pad down on the desk and sits down in the office chair. He alternates looking between the Operator and Lucy. "Well, whoever made you guys has some serious skills."

Lucy laughs.

"And I'm guessing neither of you can just take off your skin and walk around like the naked silver guys."

"Nope," the Operator says.

"And even if *we* did, they'd still see *you*."

"Let's hope we don't run into more then," Jacinto says.

"Then keep your hands off of random rooms," the Operator says, leveling a stern glance at the young hacker. "You too," he adds, looking at Lucy.

Lucy gives him a look of mock innocence, then nods.

"The cafeteria is close, right?" the Operator says to Jacinto.

"We're almost there," Jacinto says, standing up from the chair and leading the way.

They go through two more hallways before seeing the double doors up ahead. Jacinto walks tall at the front of the group until they get close, when the Operator pulls him back and takes the lead.

"What was that for?" Jacinto says, readjusting his stretched shirt collar.

"Shh," the Operator says. "I think I saw a head. Stay back," he says, walking forward with sudden caution. Taller than Jacinto, he can see inside from farther away.

At the double doors, he looks through the small square of glass at face height. Inside the cafeteria are rows and rows of standing, inert androids, the same model as the one at the check-point at the end of the tunnel from the island resort. They have blasters attached to their hips, and straps slung over their shoulders with the barrels of blaster rifles pointing to the ceiling behind their heads. The folded cafeteria tables are lined up against the left-hand wall, and there's a menacing metal door across the room.

The Operator crouches down and retreats the few steps back to Lucy and Jacinto. "Dozens of security androids," he reports.

"The same ones as the resort?" Lucy asks, her forehead wrinkled with worry.

"No, they don't have the same weapons as those guys."

Lucy's face relaxes.

"But each one has a blaster rifle and pistol."

Jacinto pulls out his data pad.

"Is there another way to the control room?" the Operator asks.

"Already on it." A moment later, the hacker shakes his head. "Nope, this is the only way without coming in from above."

"Can we do that?"

Jacinto shows the Operator a three-dimensional rendering of the building's exterior with numerous moving dots. "Not really, I was just saying it because it sounded good in the moment."

The Operator glares at him.

"Wait, are they even functional? They're just standing there, right?" Jacinto asks.

"No movement whatsoever."

"Then maybe they won't notice if we walk by."

"Or maybe they're like the android at the end of the tunnel: motion-activated."

The Operator thinks for a moment. "Jacinto, come with me," he says. When he sees Lucy look confused, he tells her she can come too.

They go into the nearest office. "Plug in," the Operator says.

Jacinto takes out his data pad and cord, then connects them to the computer. "What now?"

"Can you see all the androids in the cafeteria?"

"Sure, now that I'm looking for them."

"Can you see if they're motion-activated?"

"Why don't you just disable them like you did the one downstairs?" Lucy asks.

"I can't unplug without giving them data to report, that's why I set up the loop for the last two minutes for the one downstairs."

"You can't do it again?"

Jacinto looks at Lucy like she's crazy. "Do you know how long that would take?"

"Are they motion-activated!" the Operator growls.

"I . . . I can't tell."

"Great. Just great," the Operator says, frustrated.

They all think for a moment.

"What if we test if they're motion-activated? We could be spinning our wheels here," Jacinto offers.

"I thought about that, but I don't want to risk waking one up and the rest of the room turns on."

"Well, how long do we have after you unplug before the

androids recover from being disabled?" Lucy asks. When Jacinto looks at her, she adds, "Without the loop."

"Beats me," Jacinto says, dismissing the idea.

"Is there a way you can find out?" the Operator asks.

Jacinto thinks for a moment. "Maybe . . . maybe I could disable them, then unplug at a specific time. Then, plug back in and see when they start reporting data again. That would be the time it takes to connect back to the network—no way that's enough to trigger an alarm."

"Test it," the Operator says.

Jacinto runs the operation and determines he has, at most, thirty seconds before the androids are back online. He peeks outside the room, looks in the cafeteria's direction, and whistles.

"It'll be close."

"Me and you can go when it's disabled, then he can follow after he unplugs," Lucy says to the Operator.

Jacinto nods. The Operator laughs.

"And what, have him walk away with us on the other side of the androids and no hope of cracking Jirasek's network from the control room? No. I'll stay with him, you go across."

Lucy looks at Jacinto with disappointment.

"No faith," Jacinto says, his head hanging.

Jacinto disables the androids and the Operator watches Lucy enter the cafeteria with bated breath. From the door, he sees her tiptoe across the room and get to the metal door opposite him. She tries the handle but it doesn't turn.

"It's locked," she mouths from across the room.

"Jacinto, can you open the door on the far side of the cafeteria," the Operator yells out to the hacker in the distant office.

"One second . . . Try now!"

Lucy pushes and walks through, closing the door but making sure it stays open a crack.

The Operator walks back to Jacinto. "You ready?"

Jacinto takes a few deep breaths and nods.

"In three . . . two . . . one . . . now!"

Jacinto rips the cord from the computer and stuffs it, along with his data pad, into his pocket. The Operator positions the hacker in front of him, and together they run down the hallway and burst into the cafeteria. With his hand on the young hacker's back, he feels the ragged breaths becoming more desperate, and he slows down while making sure Jacinto keeps moving.

"I can't—"

"You can!"

They run past the rows of gleaming silver androids, the Operator between them and Jacinto. When they get close to the door, the Operator twists his body and grabs on to the front of Jacinto's shirt with his left hand. Then, he throws the hacker through before diving through himself.

CHAPTER TWENTY-TWO

Lucy shuts the door without making a sound as soon as the Operator slides through. She listens for noise from the other side with the Operator and Jacinto.

They don't hear anything.

"That was close," Lucy says. "I counted to twenty-nine."

Jacinto looks at his data pad. "It was twenty-eight seconds," he reports.

The Operator and Jacinto stand up and dust themselves off. The area beyond the thick metal door has walls with a thin layer of metal grating covering wall-mounted guns and axes.

"They're prepared for trouble," the Operator says, inspecting the weapons. There are enough blaster pistols and rifles for the inert androids in the cafeteria and some reinforcements.

"There's the stairs," Jacinto says, pointing to a break in the wall on their right. The trio climb up the steps to two doors blocking access to the hundredth level. There's a small screen on the right side of the door.

"I wonder whose face unlocks it," Jacinto says, looking for somewhere he can plug in his data pad. A crease appears between his eyebrows. "It doesn't have a plug." He looks at Lucy and the Operator.

Lucy shrugs.

The Operator looks at the concrete wall around the screen. "Could you go in through the wires?" he asks.

"Sure, if there were any."

The Operator withdraws his blaster and fires a series of shots to the right and left of the space right above the screen. Then, he hits the new concrete edge with the butt of his blaster. When a crack forms between the two channels made with his blaster fire, he inserts his fingers into one edge and starts prying the concrete off in large chunks.

"Stop," Jacinto says when there's a sizable hole right above the screen. "There's no way they put the wires any deeper than that. They must run up from below."

The Operator sighs, then repeats the process below the screen. While he's pulling at chunks of ruined concrete, his fingers pull on a plastic-coated wire.

"Could you crush that concrete so you don't ruin the wires?" Lucy asks.

The Operator looks at Jacinto and the hacker nods. He clears more of the concrete around the wires before hitting the concrete with his blaster. It crumbles away, exposing an open area with numerous colored wires running through—other than the wires on the far left and right, none are caught in concrete.

When the Operator steps back, Jacinto steps forward and inspects the circuitry. "Didn't need those two anyways," he says after inspecting the two wires retrieved from the concrete. "They're probably trip wires, in case someone took a more . . . aggressive approach to the wall." The hacker's fingers work through the jumble, searching. He strips away the outer covering of two using a fingernail, then bends them halfway through the exposed area. Then, he inserts the two exposed points into the plug leading to his data pad.

"It worked," he says as he begins typing with one hand while he pushes the plug forward with the other, keeping the stripped wires in place. Moments later, the doors slide into the wall on their right and left.

The control room has a main terminal on the far wall. Buttons and dial-covered panels extend from the wall on each side of a single chair, with monitors and more buttons on the wall ahead. A waist-high series of servers runs through the center of the room, with more servers on the wall to their left, surrounded by metal grating like the weapons cache below.

When the trio walk inside, they discover a wide window on the right wall. The glass is thick, with fine metal mesh embedded within. Jirasek's ship hovers over the city in the distance.

"Take down the network and that thing will be a sitting duck," Jacinto says, walking around the servers and towards the main terminal.

"That's the plan," the Operator replies.

Jacinto sits down, makes a show of cracking his knuckles, and leans over the controls. "Let's see what we're working with." The controls light up, and the monitor in front of Jacinto turns from black to bright blue, with room for a password.

"Thought so," Jacinto says, pulling out his data pad. He plugs it into the control panel and starts typing.

Then stops when the alarm begins.

"It knows I'm trying to get inside," Jacinto says.

The sound of pounding on the metal door echoes through the staircase and into the control room. "I think—"

"Those guys came online? Sounds like it."

The alarm stops but the pounding continues. "Looks like

they're controlled from the ship—I can't disable them anymore. Think you guys can take care of them? This could take a while."

The Operator looks at Lucy. Despite her obvious uncertainty, she flexes her jaw and nods.

"Stay here," the Operator says. He runs through the control room and back down the stairs, clearing two at a time. Blaster fire against the door adds to the noise. The Operator shoots at the weapons cache lock and pries the metal grating using his full weight, creating an opening above the bent covering. He reaches in and grabs two blaster rifles and a blaster pistol before a loud pop pulls his attention back to the door.

There, running from the ceiling to the floor, is a crack in the thick metal, right in the center of the door.

The Operator takes the weapons back up the stairs, handing a blaster rifle to Lucy and slinging one over his shoulder. He sets the retrieved blaster pistol on the control panel near Jacinto. "This one's for you—just in case."

Jacinto nods, absorbed in the numbers streaming across his data pad.

"Are you close?" the Operator asks.

"To taking down the network of the most powerful corporation in the city? No, not quite. Need more time than that."

"Can you seal these doors again?" the Operator asks, pointing to the doors at the top of the steps that lead into the control room.

Jacinto looks at the doors, annoyed. "Those? Yes, of course. Now?"

"No," the Operator says. "Wait until I tell you." He looks at Lucy. She's holding the blaster rifle like she hasn't used one before, like she didn't hip-fire one during the battle for Chance in Sigma district.

"Set up behind the servers," the Operator says. "And shoot every android that makes it to the top of the stairs." With a hand on her shoulder, he leads her over to the best spot ahead of the staircase and helps her rest her blaster rifle on the appropriate server.

With a small explosion, the metal door snaps.

The Operator rushes forward, sliding face-first to the uppermost stair while pulling the blaster rifle from his shoulder. As soon as the bottom landing comes into view, he fires three quick shots and hits three silver android heads. They crumple to the ground. The androids behind the fallen turn the corner with their blasters aimed ahead, shuffling forward and moving their off-line comrades out of their way with their powerful steps. They receive the Operator's next shots, their bodies adding to the pile between the android attackers and the steps.

"How's it going back there?" the Operator yells between volleys.

"About halfway done," Jacinto calls back. "Maybe a little more."

"I'm fine too," Lucy calls out.

The Operator shakes his head, suppressing a chuckle, as he takes the heads off two more androids.

Jirasek's silver androids stop pressing the stairs. A moment later, a thick red liquid hits the ceiling and the wall opposite their position, and covers the fallen androids. It ignites and burns, emitting an ultrabright white light that blinds the Operator.

He pulls back, through the hacked door, and takes up a position just inside, peeking around the side with his blaster rifle aimed just above the topmost stair. From there, the white light trickles up but doesn't blind him.

"Get ready," he says to Lucy, without taking his eyes from the staircase.

For the second time, the Operator fires three quick blaster shots and hits three android heads. There's a crash as they fall down the stairs, taking other androids with them. The next wave presents five androids, approaching at a breakneck pace. He hits two but three make it to the top. He pulls out his blaster pistol and fires at the remaining androids, the lower-caliber weapon opening small holes in their chests and forcing them back but not knocking them over.

"A little help here!" the Operator yells, running forward and kicking one in the chest, sending it crashing back down the stairs. He ducks down before the androids on the lower stairs shoot him.

Two rifle shots ring out and the other two fall down as well.

The Operator retreats back to the control room side of the door. "About time," he says to Lucy.

She nods, breathing in and out through puffed-up cheeks.

"Target practice," the Operator reminds her.

Lucy nods, taking aim once more and firing another round into an exposed android head.

The Operator has a moment where he believes they can take out the entire attacking android force. He's hopeful as he shoots another round of androids with Lucy's help. Then, the red liquid appears from somewhere farther down the steps, beyond his field of vision. It hits the top of the doorframe and the walls on both sides.

"Jacinto, close these doors!" the Operator says, standing up and running around the servers via the far side of the room so he isn't exposed to the enemy.

"On it," the hacker replies. "We're almost there."

The fire already burns bright when the Operator gets to Lucy's side. Together, they fire into the doorway without seeing their targets until the door closes with a resounding slam.

The androids on the other side of the door start pounding at the door with their fists and shooting it with their blasters. With his eyes still burning, the Operator steps back from the servers and approaches Jacinto. "How long unti—"

The sound of blaster fire from *inside* the control room cuts his question short. He turns around and sees Lucy sitting on the ground, her back against the server and taking deep, calming breaths.

"There's—" she mutters, pointing to the still-closed control room door. The Operator peers over the server rack and sees two android torsos crawling forward, their legs cut off by the closing door. They each have a blaster pistol in one hand and their eyes search the area they can see above the servers. One spots the Operator's eyes and fires at him, missing as the intended target ducks down.

The Operator walks around the servers with his blaster rifle at his shoulder. As soon as he turns the corner, he fires two shots into two android skulls. He walks forward and steps on their backs, firing a handful of shots into each of their heads from behind with his blaster pistol.

With the rest of Jirasek's androids still making noise outside of the control room door, Lucy peers over the servers. The Operator meets her gaze. "Won't be a problem anymore," he says.

Lucy sets the blaster rifle on the servers like it's a heated piece of metal she wants out of her hands.

The Operator jumps back over the servers and approaches Jacinto. "How we doin'?" he asks.

"Just about there," the hacker replies.

"And these guys will turn off without commands from the ship?" Lucy asks, pointing over her shoulder with her thumb.

"Hope so. If not . . ."

"We could be in for a wild one," the Operator says.

The control room doors crack open with a groan. Numerous

wiggling silver fingers appear between the doors, pulling in both directions.

"You should pick that back up," the Operator says to Lucy, looking at the blaster rifle on the server. He shoulders his own rifle and takes aim at the widening crack. He's about to shoot when Jacinto says the network is down.

"Ship's no longer connected to the tower. No more defenses," he says with pride.

The androids continue pulling the doors.

"And what about them?" Lucy calls out while aiming at the door.

"Oh, right," Jacinto says. After a series of keystrokes on his data pad, he adds, "That's not good."

"What?" the Operator says.

"Well. I can't disable them, as you can see." The door opens to the width of a forearm. Lucy and the Operator shoot whatever androids stand in the exposed space, but the door doesn't shut.

One appears coming from the stairs as if in slow motion. Neither the Operator nor Lucy shoot as they watch the odd approach.

"All I can do is slow them down," Jacinto explains. "They won't shoot you anymore, or me for that matter, but I can't disable them. As soon as I unplug, we're targets again."

"And let me guess—they're back to full speed."

"Correct."

The Operator looks at Lucy. "We need to get to that ship," he says, turning his attention back to Jacinto.

Jacinto turns his chair around. "Already found a way. Hope neither of you has a problem with small spaces," the hacker says with a smile.

CHAPTER TWENTY-THREE

"THIS SHOULD BE IT," the Operator whispers. He and Lucy are at a vertical corner inside the large air vent that cools the servers, where they dropped down from above. The air vent continues towards a square opening on the building's surface in the distance, blocked by thin horizontal bars. They wait for a moment, listening for signs that anyone heard them.

"How are we going to get through without anyone hearing us?" Lucy whispers.

"Let's hope they're too busy dealing with the control room," the Operator says. He thinks about Jacinto in there, alone, and wonders if the hacker can find a way out. If he does, maybe they'll see each other after this is all over. The Operator pulls out his blaster pistol and fires a round into the corner of the air vent, opening a hole.

He looks through. Seeing no one around, he places the muzzle against the vent and fires again, creating space for a few of his fingers. Using his left hand, he pulls at the thin metal, aware that he could cut himself with one false move. There's a vague awareness that whatever pain he feels isn't real—since he's an android—but the programmed self-preservation doesn't retreat because of logic.

After making an open strip in the vent's thin metal, he inserts the heel of his boot into the space.

"Face the other way and brace," he tells Lucy before lining up with his back against hers. Then, he pushes with his leg, propagating the strip towards the vertical shaft they fell from.

Using a combination of careful pulls with his hands and pushes with his sturdy boots, the Operator creates enough room for their bodies. There's just one problem: the drop to the floor below is two full levels.

The port is smaller than the one Dr. Howl occupies. There's enough room for two industrial hovercrafts, or a handful of smaller vehicles. With his head through the opening, the Operator sees two sleek hovercrafts, similar to the ones in the Dominguez brothers' garage but with covered roofs. The rest of the port's floor is empty, including the space below the hole in the air vent. There's a mechanic working on one of the vehicles, and the rest of the occupants are in the far corner, either sorting through cargo or logging it on a clipboard. The Operator turns his head and looks at the closest wall. There's a hanging maroon banner with Jirasek's logo in the middle, a large black *J* overlaid on a shield with dark gray circuitry patterned on white.

The Operator withdraws back to the vent and lays out the plan for Lucy. "I'll hang from the opening, jump to the banner, and slide down. If anyone sees me, I'll take care of them before you come down the same way."

Lucy maneuvers past the Operator and looks at the banner. "You sure that will hold?" she asks.

"Not sure, but hopeful," he replies, trading positions with her once more. He bends the edges of the metal so he won't cut himself, then lowers himself through the opening.

"Wish me luck," he says before his head leaves the vent

"Good luck," Lucy whispers.

The Operator swings twice, gaining momentum. He releases his hold on the air vent on the third swing, flying through the air and grabbing a hold of the banner as he falls. It goes taut and holds as he slides down to the floor. His blaster is in his hand as soon as he's balanced, looking at the mechanic and supply specialists. Neither of them noticed him, and he hurries to a nearby stack of pallets.

He looks up at Lucy and sees the fear on her face, recognizable even from a distance. She looks at the banner and takes a deep breath before lowering herself through the opening. Hanging from the air vent, she swings once, twice . . .

And the metal tears with a loud rip. She's suspended midair for a moment, a look of complete shock on her face, before she starts falling towards the concrete floor two stories beneath her. She's not quite horizontal, but close, and her arms and legs flail as she grasps at the air around her.

The Operator starts running forward without regard for Jirasek's employees in the port, but there's little he can do given his starting distance.

Halfway to the port floor, Lucy turns over and stares at the mechanic working on the hovercraft. Her hands reach out to the ground below, her knees bent. While the Operator watches in surprise, Lucy lands on all fours, catlike, on the concrete floor. Without missing a beat, she scrambles to her feet and withdraws her blaster, firing a shot at the mechanic, then eliminates the man holding the clipboard.

"Don't shoot!" a terrified voice yells out from behind the half-disassembled cargo.

If Lucy hears them, she doesn't act like it. She storms forward, her blaster held in front of her.

The Operator grabs hold of Lucy and spins her around. He

stares into her expressionless face, recognizing the mask from the shoot-out at Chance, while her eyes pull towards her targets.

"Don't," he says.

Lucy tries twisting away but the Operator holds her fast. "Look at me," he urges. She tries pulling away again without success. Her eyes turn to the Operator—a cold, driven gaze.

For a moment, he wonders if he's now become her target.

Then, Lucy's face relaxes and her eyes crinkle at the corners. She sees the Operator, then looks at the hole in the air vent up above. "What . . . what happened?"

"Your programming took over when you started falling."

Something pulls Lucy's attention from the direction of the surviving workers. The Operator follows her gaze while his hand reaches for his blaster.

Jirasek's surviving employees have their hands over their heads, their eyes just above the boxes of cargo. "Let us go—we'll say we never saw you."

Lucy looks at the two fallen employees, the blaster in her hand, and the Operator's blaster in his holster. "Did I . . ."

The Operator nods, then surveys the eliminated men. There's a blaster next to each man's right hand. "And a good thing you did. Looks like they were getting ready to attack." Looking at the men pleading for release, the Operator tilts his head towards the door on the back side of the port. They run, and he walks over and checks the rest of the port, making sure there aren't any stragglers.

Lucy hasn't moved when he returns to her side. "Come on," he says, gesturing to the second hovercraft in the port, the one the mechanic wasn't working on. When she approaches, he asks if she's all right.

"I'm fine. Waking up just takes a second—it's weird losing chunks of time."

"At least it went by quickly," the Operator says, looking inside the hovercraft.

"Easier than last time," Lucy mutters.

The Operator turns back to Lucy with a determination in his eyes. "You ready for this?" he says.

Lucy nods. "Enough running."

The Operator climbs into the driver's seat and Lucy gets into the passenger side. "Defenses are down, time to get on board," the Operator says. They both fasten their seat belts, and the Operator places a hand on Lucy's headrest while he backs out of the port.

Storm clouds gather overhead. Jirasek's ship hovering over the city is an enormous version of the troop carrier that Yoshiko's team took out in Gamma, itself a larger version of the sentinel: a shimmering blue-green metal ovoid. Just like the troop carrier, there's an opening on the long side. Except, instead of being just large enough for the gleaming silver androids, the large opening on the ship above the city is a full port.

The approach from Jirasek Tower brings the floating port into view from its left side. Eight rows of sentinels sit waiting for their orders, commands that won't come after Jacinto disabled Jirasek's network.

The Operator wonders how Felipe Jirasek, the man who released the city against Lucy, is handling the loss of his network. He imagines the face he saw displayed on the billboard yelling orders at his helpless techs, wondering how and why he can't control his forces. Somehow, knowing Jacinto is a kid who can't get a date makes the situation taste sweeter.

He scans the port as they get closer, looking for somewhere he can park the hovercraft—there's enough space for his smaller vehicle between the rows of sentinels. From there, he and Lucy can fight their way to Jirasek. The Operator turns towards Lucy, wondering if she realizes her programming will take over again in a few short moments.

When he turns back to the port, he sees a single sentinel hovercraft leaving the port. It's the same type that shot down Pavlova's hovercraft in Sigma, so he knows the destruction the single craft can produce. Behind it, another starts forward. Then, a third.

"They're still online!" Lucy says. She panics. "This is exactly what happened when my team got here last time," she says through heavy breaths. "We dodged these, and a missile came from the main ship."

On cue, a heavy barrel rises up on the main ship's exterior. "The ship's network must be independent," the Operator says.

All three nimble hovercrafts turn towards the Operator and Lucy's vehicle.

"They still have control! Think Pavlova lied to us? Or Jacinto?"

"They might not have known the networks were separate. Doesn't matter," the Operator says, plunging the vehicle down towards the city below. A shot from one of the attackers flies through the air where the hovercraft was moments before.

The Operator's hovercraft doesn't have any weapons, but he manages a complex series of dives, twists, turns, and speed changes while evading the three attacking hovercrafts and the missiles fired by the main ship. There's a moment when he sees the port ahead, with the three nimble vehicles left in his wake, and he believes in his own imminent landing.

Until another three sentinels come online and start lining up his vehicle in their sights.

The Operator watches his chance slip away as he banks hard to the left, avoiding a fresh wave of fire. Doing so puts him square in the sights of one of the first three chasing hovercrafts, and their shots hit the back of his vehicle, the sound of piercing metal filling the cabin.

"We're going down," the Operator says to Lucy. His words have the matter-of-fact quality of a simple fact or statement, as if he's remarking on the height of a building or facts about his preferred weapon.

He still has a modicum of control over their direction, and somehow he avoids any further shots from the attacking hovercrafts.

"We were so close," Lucy says, looking at the port retreating into the distance. "They're not following us," she reports.

"Good. I need to land this thing—it won't stay in flight much longer." The Operator scans the horizon. There's another tall building a block behind Jirasek Tower. He starts in that direction, grateful for the sputtering control.

Until Lucy yells out, "Incoming!" just before a loud explosion rocks the hovercraft.

They start spinning from the sky. Lucy's hands spread apart, bracing herself against the center console and door. The Operator holds on to the steering wheel with both hands, fighting their momentum.

During one of their rotations, the Operator sees the sentinels lined up, facing his direction, watching him fall. When he next sees them, they are in a straight line while they fly back towards the main ship, as if they had seen this movie before and know the ending.

They approach the top of Jirasek Tower, complete with security drones perched on the exterior and numerous turrets on the roof. The defenses should be inert—since Jacinto took the network off-line—but they all thought the same thing about Jirasek's ship's defenses, and look how that turned out.

No longer concerned with being blasted from the sky courtesy of the ship, the Operator angles their descent while aiming at the front edge of the tower. He waits for the activation of the turrets, but they don't move as the hovercraft descends towards the top of Jirasek Tower.

The last thing he sees is the roof's gray concrete taking up his entire field of vision.

CHAPTER TWENTY-FOUR

THE FIRST THING the Operator hears is the crackle of electricity surrounding him. His eyes open and he sees the stolen hovercraft's blurred wreckage. He closes his eyes again and lets out a groan. The seat belt digs into his shoulder when he tries sitting up, pinning him to the seat. With his eyes still closed, he reaches across his body and fumbles with the locking mechanism. There's a noticeable lack of grip strength when he tries pressing the button, but he unlocks it with an added effort. Without the seat belt holding him in place, he collapses into the center console.

He opens his eyes again and waits until they focus. Everything is at a forty-five-degree angle through the spider-webbed windshield. The building he flew towards before being shot down is off in the distance, surrounded by dark clouds. Inside the hovercraft, the damaged electronics on the dashboard sizzle and crack. Looking at Lucy, he sees a trickle of blood on her forehead. Maneuvering his body so he can use the arm closest to her, he reaches over, finds her seat belt clasp, and releases the strap. She falls limp against the passenger-side window.

Another groan escapes the Operator's lips as he engages his

abdominal muscles and reaches for his door. He pulls on the latch and hears the lock disengage but the door doesn't move, pinned down by its own weight with the angle of their crashed vehicle. Pushing on the door with his arm doesn't work. He turns in his seat and puts his lower back against the center console while pulling his knees to his chest. The memory of sitting back-to-back with Lucy in the vent flashes through his mind—it seems like a lifetime ago. He extends his legs against the door, braces himself, and pushes.

At first, the door still doesn't move. It opens a crack with a continued effort that leaves him gasping. He starts kicking the door, first with one foot, then with both, prying the door open a bit more each time. On the final kick, the door flies open and stays stuck in its position, misaligned with the vehicle's frame.

The Operator climbs out and collapses on the ground in a heap. There's a path of destruction through the various machines dotting Jirasek Tower's roof: bent antennae and leveled climate-control units. The wrecked hovercraft rests against a large complex of metal box-shaped machines on a raised platform near the edge of the roof—the sole barrier to their continued path off the edge and into the hundred-story fall beyond. The Operator uses the various pipes and metal underneath the hovercraft for support on his way to standing. Then, he climbs back onto the hovercraft, resting his stomach on the bottom of the doorframe so he can reach inside.

"Lucy!" he yells, his voice hoarse. He coughs, clearing his throat. "Lucy!" he calls again.

There's no response.

The Operator shuffles forward until he's worried about falling in. Then, he reaches out and slams a hand against the center console. Lucy doesn't stir. He yells her name, punctuated by a hit on the center console, over and over until she moves her head.

"Come on, you can do it," he says.

She opens and closes her eyes again and again until a look of sudden realization covers her face and her eyes stay wide open. Her world focuses, and she looks at the Operator. "Leave me in here. I'm done."

The Operator's mouth hangs open while he processes the information. "What are you talking about?" he says after recovering from his shock. He reaches into the space between them. "Give me your hand."

Lucy looks at the Operator. "No."

"Why not?" the Operator says, letting his hand fall to the driver's seat and using it for support.

Lucy sighs. "We failed. *I* failed, twice now. It's impossible."

"No it's not, we just need to figure—"

"There's nothing else we can do! What don't you understand?"

The Operator thinks for a moment.

"Why don't you climb out; we can talk about it out here."

Lucy looks at the hovercraft's dashboard. "I remember who I am. Who I *was*, before falling from the sky."

The Operator stares at her, waiting.

"I'm a cyber weapon. A virus, made for Jirasek's ship." She looks at the Operator. "You know how Jacinto had to stay plugged in so we could escape?"

The Operator nods.

"Well, I was going to do the same thing hovering above the city. Stay plugged in and go down with the ship while the rest of the squadron escaped."

The Operator lets the information digest. A loud noise from behind him demands his attention. He scrambles out from the wreckage and turns his head.

Jirasek's androids stream onto the roof through a door on the far side. The slam was the door hitting the wall behind as it flew open.

The androids in front take cover behind the closest machines, and as more come onto the roof they expand and disappear behind cover farther and farther away from the door. The Operator rushes forward as fast as his broken body allows and hides behind a solid-looking metal cube with a high-voltage sticker. Peeking out from the side, he fires a series of shots into the open door, exploding an android's head before their body falls back down the approaching stairs. He ducks back behind cover a split second before an android with a clear shot on him pulls the trigger.

Grateful his blaster pistol inflicts damage on these androids —unlike the elite ones in Gamma who just stumbled when shot —he pops his head over the cube and fires two quick shots at two exposed androids before ducking behind cover once more.

The Operator alternates appearing from all three sides of the cube, firing a few shots before the androids' focused fire forces him back. Twice in a row, he can't even get a shot off. Reinforcements stream in from the doorway and their ever-expanding wave of taken ground creeps towards his location.

He's wondering about how he could lure them to his current location and blow up a large group of them when the sound of continuous blaster fire reaches his ears—none of the shots reach his chosen cover. He looks past the edge of the cube closest to the noise.

And sees Lucy walking forward, her blaster pistol held with a straight arm in front of her chest. It's unlike anything he's ever seen—she was fast in Chance, but now she's also anticipating incoming shots. The slimmest sliver of android heads popping up over cover get taken off before their full face is in view. She twists when two appear at the same time, dodging the first android's shot while shooting the second, then contorting her body while shooting the other. It's as if she has the fastest computation system ever created and her body is an extension of those decisions.

After clearing the field of androids, she closes the door, walks over to the Operator, and kneels down next to him. He expects the same trancelike state he saw in the club—and for a second in the port—but she seems the same, recognizing him with a slight smile.

"Jacinto must've left," she says. "There will be more."

"What made you change your mind?" the Operator asks.

"I'm helping you get off this tower," she says with grim resolve.

The Operator nods. "Thanks."

"Don't mention it."

"But I'm not going anywhere without you."

The two of them look at each other in frustration, each stubborn in their own way.

The door slams open in the distance. Lucy leans back and fires her blaster at the door without ever breaking eye contact.

"And what's going on? You're . . . still here," the Operator says, pointing to her eyes.

"Even though I don't want to be. I'm tired of remembering; I just want to go back to before I woke up."

"So you're trying to become mindless and you can't. Before you didn't want to and you would," the Operator says, grinning.

"Funny how it works out like that."

Numerous footsteps ring out across the roof. Both the Operator and Lucy pop over the metal cube and take out the androids before they can take cover.

Lucy looks at the Operator with sad eyes. "I can't handle the memories. Once we get you off of here, maybe the Enforcers can fix me, turn me back to the way I was."

The Operator blinks. His thoughts go back to Patrice, his

former fiancée, and the heartbreak that sent him into the badlands and changed the course of his life forever. Getting rid of her memory, if it was possible . . .

"Your memories are what make you who you are," the Operator says, both to himself and to Lucy. "Without them, you're just another android."

Lucy looks down at the concrete roof. "That's what I want."

"The Enforcers can make another android. They can't make another you." The Operator reaches out and lifts Lucy's chin. He waits until her eyes meet his. "Trust me, you're worth fighting for."

A single tear falls down Lucy's cheek. She takes a second before she nods. "Well, now I can't even forget when I want to!" she says with a laugh, wiping her eyes.

"And you're better for it. I've never even imagined doing what you can do."

Lucy laughs. "Well, I had a good reason."

The Operator feels the corners of his lips curl up. "Tell you what: Why don't we fight for each other?" he says while extending a hand.

Lucy tilts her head then shakes on the agreement.

"So, are we going to figure out another way onto Jirasek's ship?" the Operator asks with raised eyebrows.

"Let's just focus on getting off this roof," Lucy fires back.

Hooks appear at the edge of the roof beyond the wrecked hovercraft. "It doesn't look like we're going anywhere," the Operator says. Moments later, androids start climbing over the edge. Both the Operator and Lucy fire at the androids, sending them one hundred levels down to the surface. Blaster fire from the direction of the first wave zings over their heads, while some of it hits their cover.

"I'll take care of those," Lucy says, gesturing with her head towards the roof's door. "You just make sure none climb over the edge."

The Operator adopts a prone position, and together with Lucy, they fire round after round into the androids on both sides. A few of the androids the Operator shoots have managed their way onto the roof, and their bodies block his view of the hooks behind them. The androids who climb up behind them use their fallen comrades as shields, giving them time for a few shots. One hits the Operator's left arm.

"Are you all right?" Lucy calls out when she notices the Operator's sudden jerk.

The Operator presses the back of his right hand to his arm and inspects the fluid on his hand. "I'm fine," he says, firing a continuous barrage at the android who shot him. Most of the shots hit the body ahead of the android, but one finds its mark and the attacker falls from the edge.

"My shots aren't working on two of these!" Lucy says. Despite the development, her voice remains steady. "They just stumble back."

The Operator knows what's coming. He grabs Lucy and pulls her away from the door's direction as she yells out, "They're flying!"

They run around the wrecked hovercraft, then onto the complex of machines that stopped their momentum after the crash, while androids stream onto the roof. The Operator turns around and sees Jirasek's elite androids land near their former cover after the thruster-assisted jump. "Shoot the cube!" he says to Lucy.

Getting through the cube's hard metal exterior takes valuable seconds of vulnerability, even with their combined fire. The elite androids stand up and lift their right arms.

The cube explodes just before they acquire their aim.

Flames shooting high into the sky command everyone's

attention. The two elite androids are limp on the ground, limbs missing from both. Thick black smoke rises up from the former cube's location, and more standard androids appear on each side of the conflagration.

A wave of hooks appear on the roof's edge. Without speaking a word, Lucy starts firing at the androids already on the roof and the Operator focuses on the ones climbing onto it from the building's exterior.

He shoots as fast as he can, but it's no match for the speed of Lucy's continuous fire into the advancing horde.

CHAPTER TWENTY-FIVE

LYING prone in his chosen spot between two of the complex's machines, the Operator fires round after round into the androids appearing at the edge of the roof. Lucy ducks, crawls, dodges, and dances her way through the various options for cover, always coming up shooting.

"There's too many of them," she yells.

The Operator thinks the same thing. "Take out as many as you can," he responds.

"Oh, I am."

An android starts shooting at the Operator's position before climbing onto the roof. The Operator ducks down, covering his head with his hands. During a brief pause in the android's fire, he lifts his head again and shoots the now-kneeling android before it stands up. But, while he was distracted, two more androids managed their way onto the roof—they shoot at him from a kneeling position. He maneuvers around the machine on his left and takes them out. He peeks over the obstruction, and sees three more standing at their full height.

Beyond them, in the distance, sentinels stream from Jirasek's ship and turn towards his location, framed by ominous clouds.

He sits back down, leaning on his cover for support, not saying anything so Lucy doesn't worry. She'll find out soon enough. He looks at her, abandoning his task for a moment, both admiring her impressive shooting abilities and proud of her for fighting instead of giving up.

The combination of the pause in his blaster fire and the feel of his gaze turns her attention towards him. She kneels down and meets his gaze. Then, she looks up towards Jirasek's ship. Her eyes widen when she sees the sentinels speeding towards their location. She looks at him and smiles.

"As many as we can," she mouths, her words lost in the sound of incoming blaster fire.

The Operator nods.

He turns back towards the androids on the roof and throws himself to the ground between his two chosen barriers. Dozens stand still at the roof's edge, waiting with their blasters aimed in his direction. Behind and above them, the twelve sentinels sent by Jirasek's main ship form up in a rectangular pattern, three rows of four across, looking down at the last stand. The androids already on the roof stop firing, and an eerie silence descends on the roof once Lucy pauses her attack.

Jirasek's army all look at the Operator and Lucy. The Operator wipes his brow with the back of the shirtsleeve on his left forearm.

From behind and below the arranged sentinels, emerging from the shadow of a nearby building, come four hovercrafts. Their lights are off, and they streak towards Jirasek Tower through the darkened sky. When they reach the halfway mark, dozens of hovercrafts also appear from behind the building and follow the initial group.

As the Operator watches, bodies climb from the passenger seat of each of the four closest hovercrafts and take up position on the hood. When they get still closer, he sees four crouched people with exoskeletons encasing their arms and legs.

Yoshiko's Enforcers, coming out for the fight.

The hovercraft drivers raise the angle of their approach, aiming at the uppermost sentinels. Just before impact, they dive in unison. At the same instant, the four elite Enforcers jump from the hoods of the vehicles, landing on the top four sentinels. Jirasek's smallest ships shift forward at the impact before their thrusters correct their position. By then, three of the Enforcers have their shotguns pulled from their shoulder holsters—they fire round after round into the sentinels. The fourth prefers using their hands, tearing through the metal exterior and ripping the innards out, tossing them into the dark sky.

The four highest sentinels fall from the sky, taking the Enforcers with them.

The four sentinels in the lowest row take off in pursuit of the hovercrafts that transported the Enforcers, leaving just the middle row, who shifted forward when their comrades above them fell from the sky. By now, the trailing hovercrafts have come into a better view. Each one has two passengers with blasters in hand—one in the passenger seat and one on the hood. Upon closer inspection, the Operator sees the bouncers from Chance and skinless androids holding the blasters, driven by what look like random Sigma residents. They make a passing volley of initial fire before peeling off.

Despite the numerous shots that hit the four remaining sentinels, none penetrate their exterior. The attacking hovercrafts scatter as the sentinels turn and start firing.

It all happens so fast that the androids on the roof haven't even flinched. The Operator scrambles back from his prone position and looks at Lucy.

"Looks like we have some help," he says.

Lucy smiles, takes a big breath, and turns back towards the

androids on the roof, shooting with renewed energy. The androids start firing back after her first shot, drowning out the noise from the air battle taking place in the sky near Jirasek Tower.

The Operator, prone once more, starts firing round after round into the advancing androids. At first, he tries choosing the closest androids, but once he realizes they're all closing in on him, he sweeps left to right, hoping one will fall down and slow their comrades. He continues firing despite his diminishing hope as heads start disappearing from the group's rear. By the time Jirasek's androids that climbed onto the roof using hooks realize they have attackers behind them and turn around, the four Enforcers have their blaster shotguns out and are spreading metal body parts all over the roof.

"We got these guys," an Enforcer yells after they rip an android head from its body.

The Operator nods then scrambles back and shoots an android who appears on their side, unseen by Lucy. He shoots back against the flanking wave, then joins Lucy in shooting the main horde.

They work in tandem as if they've trained together for years. When Lucy drops down, the Operator shoots over her head. Twice they shoot androids that encroach on each other's position from the side. Lucy, faster than the Operator, shoots the occasional android that gets closer than she likes on his side. An android from her side aims at the Operator from the rear and she pushes him away, the shot whistling past his head.

Neither group makes progress. Lucy and the Operator can't force them back, and the androids can't get any closer. From the top of his field of vision, the Operator sees the four Enforcers descend, having jumped high in the air with the aid of their exoskeletons. They shoot androids as they fall, then roll upon impact and come up firing. The Operator and Lucy keep shooting, protecting the Enforcers from incoming blaster fire.

A sentinel chases a passenger-less hovercraft over the roof's battle, shooting it down past the edge of the building. It explodes in a fireball and falls from the sky. The sentinel flies over the Operator's head, back towards Jirasek's main ship.

The Operator watches it and turns towards the air battle behind him. He counts six remaining sentinels and far fewer hovercrafts than before. The sentinels keep chasing the hovercrafts despite being hit by blaster fire, the smaller crafts' maneuverability the main factor in their survival. Without the confines of being between buildings near the surface, and with the full range of vertical options available, Sigma's hovercrafts now have more available movement options than when the surviving Dominguez brother tried evading his sentinel attacker. No sooner than he thinks about the surviving Dominguez brother does he see the man fly by from below the roof's edge, the nose of his vehicle pointed straight to the sky—a skinless android holds on to the hood for dear life.

Without any effective weaponry for the sentinels' tough exterior, there's nothing standing between the hovercraft's destruction and the sentinels but time.

The sentinel chasing the surviving Dominguez brother explodes below the edge of the roof, the top edge of the blast sending a fireball between the Operator and the air battle. Then, through the flames, a new kind of hovercraft appears, one with a clear spherical center, a black outline for the rounded square door, and two wings. It's unlike anything the Operator's ever seen.

Sitting in the cockpit, smiling down on the Operator, is Yoshiko Apocalypse with her Hololenses on her head. There are four empty seats behind her. She nods once, puts her glasses back over her eyes, then turns her craft around and joins the dogfight. Seven more of the same model emerge from below the roof's edge, following Yoshiko for a moment before splitting off in search of the remaining six sentinels. They shoot two down before Jirasek's main ship has other ideas, sending out the other half of the sentinel forces.

"That's what we flew up on the first time," Lucy says, watching alongside the Operator. "We took the first finished one." She nudges him with her elbow, and together they turn around and help the Enforcers on the roof eliminate the remaining android forces.

When it's obvious the Enforcers will take care of what's left of the androids, the Operator turns back towards the dogfight taking place beneath the dark clouds overhead. The hovercrafts from Sigma are gone, either shot down or leaving the hard work for those with the appropriate hardware. Yoshiko and her team roll and dive away from the incoming sentinel fire in an impressive display of piloting. The main ship raises six battle turrets, tracking the new aerial threats. The pilots in the new hovercrafts dodge the incoming fire when they can, but three of the ships get stuck between being shot by the ship or by the sentinels and end up going down in flames. One of Jirasek's ship's missiles hits their own ship, exploding it in a fireball and freeing up the two pursuing spherical vehicles.

Both the sentinels and the spherical hovercrafts execute complex evasive maneuvers during their battle, but despite their best effort, the sentinels start falling one by one. Yoshiko herself takes out five of the sixteen ships. At the end of the battle, all the sentinels are gone, and the five remaining spherical hovercrafts position their vehicles with a building between themselves and Jirasek's main ship, away from the turrets.

The tops of two clear spheres appear on the far side of Jirasek Tower; the ship's turrets don't shoot at the building. The four Enforcers on the roof wave the Operator and Lucy towards the vehicles, then take off running towards the hovercrafts themselves. The Enforcers stop at the edge of the roof and wait while the Operator and Lucy catch up. There's one Enforcer that the Operator hasn't seen before.

Both hovercrafts open their hatches. "Can I give you a ride to the ship?" Yoshiko says with a sly grin.

Lucy looks at the Operator, searching for guidance. This is the same woman and the same elite team that chased them all over the city, through Gamma and Sigma, from the surface to the top of the tallest tower.

"I'll explain on the way," Yoshiko says. "Come on."

The Operator shrugs. "They did save us," he says to Lucy before climbing in.

Yoshiko looks at the four Enforcers wearing exoskeletons. "Be ready if we need you," she says. They all nod before getting into the second spherical hovercraft.

Lucy and the Operator strap themselves in, and Yoshiko emerges from around the side of the building, heading towards Jirasek's main ship. Lightning flashes ahead of them, hitting the large craft's hull and dissipating with a shimmer. A few heavy drops of water splash against the clear sphere.

"What about the missiles?" Lucy says with trepidation in her voice.

"Oh, those? We have sensors on board this model. Not a problem at all."

"You didn't have sensors on the one that got shot down?" the Operator asks.

"Didn't know Jirasek had such extensive defenses," Yoshiko replies, her voice level, as if stating a fact.

Jirasek's ship fires at the approaching hovercraft. An onboard sensor detects the projectile and executes corrective action without input from the pilot. "Quite a first ride for the new Enforcer," Yoshiko says as the hovercraft dodges an incoming missile. She doesn't mention that the Operator is the one who shot the previous fifth member of her team.

"Thanks for showing up," the Operator says after an uncomfortable moment when neither he nor Lucy replies. One question still lingers for him, scratching at the back of his skull. "If we want the same thing, why were you chasing us around the city?"

Yoshiko keeps her eyes on the fast-approaching port. "Do you know what she is?" she asks the Operator, referring to Lucy.

"A cyber weapon," Lucy says.

"Made to completely destroy the digital infrastructure she plugs into. The plan works because Jirasek is notorious for his independent network—"

"*Networks*—his tower and ship are separate."

Yoshiko continues as if the interruption never happened. "And we couldn't have her infecting the entire city. You think Jirasek ground the city to a halt? Just imagine if *everything*—power, water, the reclaimers—stopped working."

The Operator looks at Lucy. She nods with solemnity.

The hovercraft dodges three consecutive missiles, the last-gasp defenses of an exposed ship.

"You two ready to do this?" Yoshiko says, angling towards the port's floor.

CHAPTER TWENTY-SIX

Yoshiko glides the spherical hovercraft into the empty port, setting it down with a gentle thud. Two thin poles at the ends of the wings snap into place before the stabilizing thrusters turn off. The Operator, Lucy, and Yoshiko climb from the vehicle and adopt a shooting position as soon as their feet hit the ground. A crack of thunder overhead breaks the eerie calm throughout the expansive space as heavy rain blurs the rest of the city.

"Just in time," Lucy says, looking outside.

Wondering why the parked hovercraft doesn't tip over, the Operator looks beneath the sphere and discovers two nondescript black triangles next to the thrusters that work as wedges. "Let's go," he says to the other two members of the boarding party.

The port they landed in is in the center of the large blue-green ovoid. The ship, hovering in place since its first appearance, never moved forward or backwards, and none of them know the location of the ship's bridge. The Operator suggests they travel towards the side farthest away from Jirasek Tower.

Lucy and Yoshiko agree, and they run across the port and through a retracting door in the middle of the bare beige wall.

The halls are painted bright white and appear abandoned. "Watch out for booby traps," Yoshiko says. There are air ducts dotted throughout the upper wall, large spaces similar to the one the Operator traveled through with Lucy. "Keep an eye on those," the Operator whispers.

They move through the ship with a pause at each aisle they cross. No defenses, and no attackers.

"Where is everyone?" Lucy whispers.

In the silence after her question, the trio hears a panel sliding behind them. They all turn around and watch as a silver android arm appears from an opening near the ground. Three blasters aim at the emerging android head—the Operator fires first, leaving the limp android body half-exposed in the hall.

"One of us has to walk backwards," Yoshiko says. After a moment's pause, she adds, "I'll do it."

The Operator and Lucy, with Yoshiko watching their back, continue on their path to the end of the ship. The aisle connecting to the port doesn't run the ship's length—when one hallway ends, they turn towards the ship's center line before finding another one heading in their desired direction. Yoshiko takes out three androids that appear behind them, and the Operator springs into action when two appear ahead of them, one from a wall panel next to the ground and one from the vents. At long last, they find a hall that ends with a door instead of a wall.

"Should be getting close," Yoshiko says. "This might be it."

"Are you ready?" the Operator asks Lucy.

She grips her blaster with both hands and joins Yoshiko in standing next to the left wall. "Ready."

The Operator, next to the right wall, pushes a square button on the wall and the door flies open. It's a large, open space, running all the way to the top of the ship, with rows of desks with computers in the center. There's a kitchen space on the right side, and various exercise equipment on the left. On the back wall, the same number of haggard humans as there are desks stare at the three intruders from where they sit on makeshift cots. Thin cables with curtains on rings run above and between the sleeping areas, the curtains all pressed into corners.

"Don't shoot!" a man with a bushy beard says while standing up, his hands in the air. At a gesture from him, the rest of the humans raise their hands as well. There's something familiar about his face that the Operator can't quite place.

"Where's Jirasek?" Yoshiko asks when the three of them get closer to the cots, her blaster still held perpendicular from her body.

"That . . . that is Jirasek," Lucy says. "He's the one from the billboard."

The Operator imagines the man with a much shorter beard and realizes she's right: Jirasek the coward, hiding with his hostages. He lunges forward, grabs the man by the back of the neck, and aims the blaster at his head. "Tell us how to take the ship down," he snarls.

"What are you talking about?" the terrified man squeaks. "I just want to get home and see my daughter, make sure she's safe."

"Lies!" the Operator says.

"Let him go, he's not going anywhere," Lucy says, her voice steady.

The Operator pushes the man back down on the cot.

"This isn't the ship's control room, is it?" Lucy continues, looking around.

"No, we've been taking care of the company from up here," the man says while staring at the Operator's blaster still aimed at his face.

"We didn't have a choice!" a woman three cots over yells.

Lucy turns to the Operator. "Remember how Jacinto had a different image for his official identification?"

The Operator nods, at first unsure why she's bringing up the fact. Then, with a sudden realization, he asks the man if he ever spoke to the city's citizens for help finding a woman. "No, I've been stuck in here! We weren't allowed to send any messages once we took flight."

"If Jirasek wanted to use one of your faces for a broadcast— does the company have the technology for that?" Lucy asks.

"Easily," a slender man says from the back. "He has mountains of data from all of us, including hours of video. Wouldn't take him long at all."

Lucy turns to Yoshiko. "We've got to get them out of here before we take down the ship."

Yoshiko nods. "Agreed." She pulls out a handheld communication device from her pocket. She starts counting hostages before shaking her head. "All ships, come into the port."

She receives static in response.

"Doesn't work in here," Yoshiko says, looking around.

"Jammers," the slender man says, standing up. "I can get you onto the ship's network—"

He stops when he realizes the blasters are still aimed in his general direction.

Yoshiko beckons him forward with her weapon. "How long will it take?" she asks when he approaches.

"Not long at all." The employee takes the communication device from her and walks to a nearby computer as he removes the plastic cover, exposing the wires. He announces it works within a minute.

"All empty ships, land in the port. Watch for incoming missiles," Yoshiko says into the coverless device.

A tense moment passes before the device roars back to life. "Copy."

"Let's go," Yoshiko says to the group. "I'll lead the way. You two"—she points to the Operator and Lucy—"bring up the rear."

The Operator pulls the bearded man to the side. "The bridge is on the other side of the ship?" he asks.

The man nods.

"And Jirasek's there?"

Another quick nod. "With his four personal guards."

The Operator lets the man go and they both fall into their assigned positions within the traveling group. He watches the bearded man the entire walk back to the port, looking for anything suspicious; Yoshiko thwarts a single android surprise attack during the trip.

"Go," Yoshiko says to the hostages, standing aside, when they get into the port and discover the parked Enforcer hovercrafts. Water droplets cover the clear spheres and pool on the port's floor. The employees all run to the waiting ships and climb aboard. The Enforcer pilots, wearing their black Hololenses, stand in the puddles next to their vehicles and look at Yoshiko while waiting for orders. She dismisses them with a nod. They climb back into their respective ships with the rescued captives and fly off.

"Bridge was on the other side," the Operator says with a shrug when it's just the three of them again.

They cross the port and go through the door on the other side, a mirror image of their first trip into the depths of the ship. This time, as soon as the door slides open, they're met with a blast of fire. They dive to either side of the door.

"Are you all right?" Yoshiko asks the Operator and Lucy. She's on one side of the door, separated from the other two.

Lucy looks at the Operator and announces that they're fine.

The Operator crawls forward and looks into the space

beyond the door. There's a single elite android lying prone on the floor, both arms extended forward. Behind it, three more silver elites have their right arms raised at the door. They all shoot at the Operator's head when they see movement on the floor in the port; he pulls back just in time.

"Four elites," the Operator reports. "Jirasek's guard. One on the ground, three behind."

Yoshiko pulls out her communication device. "Team, stand by after ensuring hostage transport."

"Copy."

The Operator looks around. There's no other doors they can go through, and nothing he can use for cover. He mimes a message to Yoshiko, making a gun with his hands and pointing it to his arm, followed by an explosion. She nods in understanding. Then, he turns to Lucy. "The flamethrower on their arm explodes if we shoot it."

Yoshiko backs away from the door, careful she isn't seen by the defending androids. She takes a steadying breath, holds her blaster away from her body, and leans into the open space in front of the door for a brief moment, firing a single shot. There's an explosion, accompanied by flames shooting through the door. The blaster fire from the rear androids miss the lead Enforcer and hit the far side of the port.

"Wish we knew that little trick back at the resort," she says.

The Operator stands next to the door, the air around him clouded by thick black smoke. He stares at Lucy as if seeing her for the first time, then turns to Yoshiko. "Make sure she gets there," he says.

"No!" Lucy screams as the Operator turns into the flames and runs through the door.

He can't see anything through the smoke. The flames burn his legs, and once he's into the hallway he pushes his body against the left-side wall, the farthest side from the exploded flamethrower. Despite every self-preservation instinct, he jumps forward and rolls. The movement takes him to the edge of the smoke, near the incapacitated android's knees, and he shoots while diving to the right, hitting the flamethrower on the left-most android.

The middle and right androids start firing on his former position before the blast makes them stumble to their right. For a moment, the Operator wonders if the androids will retreat or press forward out of the black smoke. He sees their silver legs marching forward. From where he lies on the ground, he shoots another flamethrower, sending yet another fireball throughout the hall. The final android fires at the Operator just as someone steps over his body.

The shot hits Lucy in the leg. She falls in a heap while another shot, from the left-hand side of the hall, hits the remaining android's flamethrower and their arm explodes. The Operator covers Lucy's body with his own, the flames burning his shirt and the skin on his back. A groping hand from farther in the hall reaches the Operator and pulls him forward. He fights, holding on to Lucy.

He hears Yoshiko's muffled voice yell, "Come on!" as she pulls him off. Then, he grabs Lucy and pulls her forward. Lucy half stumbles, half crawls over the three fallen androids before collapsing into the hall beyond the smoke.

Yoshiko pulls her face from beneath her shirt and gulps air. She looks at the Operator and points at Lucy. "She . . . she followed . . ." She then reaches forward and extinguishes a piece of burning cloth on the Operator's shoulder.

The Operator looks at Lucy. "What were you thinking?" he says.

"We're fighting for each other," Lucy says with resounding stubbornness. She reaches down to her calf and presses where she got shot. Body fluids surround the hole in the singed fabric of her pants. "What were you thinking?" she asks him.

"That you need to get to Jirasek's control room."

Lucy sits up and looks at the Operator's burned pants. She turns him around with a push on his shoulder and inspects his back. "*We* have to get there."

Yoshiko has her blaster held towards the bridge in case there are other defenses on the way. "We should get moving. Can you walk?" she asks Lucy.

The Operator helps Lucy stand up. Lucy tries putting weight on the leg, but the injured limb can't accept much. "It'll be slow."

"Help her," Yoshiko says, pointing to the Operator. "I'll walk backwards, just like before."

Together, the three of them traverse to the end of the ship without any further attacks. They pause outside a door identical to the one where they found Jirasek's employees.

"The old plan involved Lucy angling the ship towards the bay and taking it down," Yoshiko says. "If you disable the ship above the city—"

"We're sticking with the old plan," Lucy says, shrugging off the Operator's assistance and standing up with a hand on the wall for support.

"Then this is where we part. I'll go back to my ship and leave you to it." She looks at the Operator. "Want a ride?"

The Operator shakes his head no. "I'm with her."

"I figured as much. Good luck," Yoshiko says before taking off back towards the port.

"You ready for this?" the Operator asks Lucy.

Lucy sets her jaw and nods. The Operator presses the square button and the door flies open.

CHAPTER TWENTY-SEVEN

THERE'S A WIDE, curved piece of glass covering the far wall overlooking the city and, in the distance, the bay outside Theta district through streaks of water. A vast array of control stations sit in front of the window, all abandoned. A raised platform halfway to the ceiling has a staircase on the left and right leading up to it, with a single control panel in the center.

And standing in front of the lone control panel is a man wearing an all-white admiral's uniform, facing the window with his hands clasped behind his back. Felipe Jirasek.

"Let me go first," the Operator says to Lucy.

The Operator walks into the ship's bridge with his blaster drawn. He looks left and right as soon as he enters, searching for threats. His left arm aches from the earlier blast shot; his legs and back scream from the fresh burns. He continues towards the bulk of the ship's controls, scanning the various displays and lights in front of empty chairs.

All of a sudden, every screen shows the scene in the bridge, the camera looking down from somewhere along the center of the window ahead of Jirasek.

"I'm coming directly to you, the citizens, to show you what

they do to those who try improving the city. This is my true identity—no more hiding." Jirasek pauses for dramatic effect. "All my employees are gone," Jirasek says with serenity, his head tilting forward. "I'm the only one left."

The Operator turns onto the left staircase and climbs up the platform. Standing on the same level as Jirasek, he realizes the man's shorter than most, with an obvious bald spot the few strands on the top of his head can't hide.

"What did you expect? A last stand? A holdout? You got past all of my best technology, there's little more I can do," Jirasek says. He turns to the Operator. "I'm just a man."

The Operator keeps his gun trained on Jirasek while he approaches him. "A man who tried to take over the city."

"Is that such a bad thing? All these petty squabbles about levels, leaving those at the surface to fend for themselves in the haze. One person in control can ensure proper resource allocation, instead of concentrated wealth at the top."

"You killed people."

"So did you!" Jirasek notices the gun and cools a degree. "The costs of improving society." Jirasek waits for a moment before looking back out the window with newfound calmness. "Those on the lower levels: you can thank the Enforcers for stripping away your chance for equality."

The Operator doesn't know if he should talk to Jirasek or to the city. "I'm not an Enforcer."

"And yet you bring their main weapon on my ship to use against me!" Jirasek snarls. "Let that be a lesson for those who manage to make something of themselves—the city won't let you succeed!"

"Are you the champion for the lower levels or for those seeking wealth and power?" Lucy yells from just inside the access door. The Operator turns towards her and watches her hobble along the center aisle, limping. Each step leaves a bloody footprint. Her eyes grow wide and she raises her blaster, planting for a fraction of a second and firing her weapon towards the platform before crumpling into a heap.

The Operator turns to Jirasek and sees the man hit the control panel with his back. A miniature blaster falls to the ground with a clang against the metal. He rushes forward and moves the blaster out of reach before searching Jirasek for more weapons. There's a growing red spot on Jirasek's side that stands in sharp contrast with his clean white uniform.

"Are you okay?" the Operator asks Lucy.

"I'm fine," Lucy says through gritted teeth. She tries standing up but stumbles with the slightest pressure on her leg.

The Operator makes Jirasek stand up then marches him down to the controls below the platform, forcing him into the center seat. The camera follows their movement—the displays show a seated Jirasek from above. The Operator runs a hand beneath the consoles around the man and finds a hidden blaster. He tosses it to the ground.

"How many of these do you have in here?" the Operator asks.

"That's the last one," Jirasek says with a mischievous twinkle in his eye, sowing doubt.

Walking backwards with his blaster aimed at Jirasek, the Operator goes back to Lucy and helps her stand up. They walk forward together while the Operator supports her with his right arm.

"Are you watching?" Jirasek says, looking up at the camera. The Operator follows his gaze and finds the small black dot against the water-covered window. "They refuse to give up power!"

"We're not the ones clinging to the takeover of a city," Lucy says, shaking her head. She looks at the camera. "Those living on the higher levels know how you ruined their businesses with your blockade. Killed innocent hovercraft drivers. And you, on the lower levels—ask yourselves what he did for you, other than give you a single chance for rising to a higher level just for capturing me. No mention of how you'd ever afford living there." She turns to Jirasek. "Well, here I am. What exactly did you want to do?"

Jirasek looks at Lucy, then at the Operator. "My success really bothers you." He turns to the camera again. "Remember this when you try and improve your lot in life."

The Operator laughs. "Always the victim." He looks at Lucy. "Should I shoot the camera?"

"No, leave it running."

Both Jirasek and the Operator watch Lucy as she forces her pinky finger sideways. It breaks apart with a loud snap at the first knuckle. Lucy holds her hand up and flexes half of her pinky finger, a short cord and plug hanging from the end.

"I remembered where it was after the crash," Lucy says to the stunned men.

The Operator rips one of the displays from the terminal and grabs the attached power cable, pulling its length from the tangle of exposed machinery. When it becomes taut, he gives it a quick yank and the plug comes out. Lucy watches the Operator try separating the cable from the display, but it won't budge.

"Wha . . . what are you going to do?" Jirasek stammers.

"Captain has to go down with the ship," the Operator says, standing behind Jirasek and looping the cable around his torso and the chair. Jirasek grunts when the cord tightens around his wound. The Operator secures the man with the display still dangling from the end of the cable, before taking two more displays from the console and using their power cords for Jirasek's arms.

"Ready?" the Operator asks Lucy.

She looks at him with fear in her eyes. "I don't know what happens after I plug in."

"Okay, we can figure it out."

"There might not be a 'we.'"

"Then *I'll* figure something out."

"Save yourself if you can—I'll give you time," Lucy says, her pinky finger hovering over the plug.

"Not without you," the Operator replies.

Lucy smiles and closes her eyes. Then, she plugs the cord at the end of her pinky finger into the control panel and jerks upright. Her eyes flutter and her limbs lock into place.

"What's going on?" a scared Jirasek asks.

"She's infecting your network. The rest of the city has nothing to worry about, since you isolated yourself up here."

Jirasek pushes against his restraints. "No! You can't!" He remembers about the camera and looks up at it again. "Think about the prosperity I brought to the city! They're erasing my life's work for their own benefit!"

The Operator rips a piece of his dirty shirtsleeve from his arm, stuffing it into Jirasek's mouth. "Just . . . stop talking," he says.

Jirasek's ship lurches forward towards the bay outside Theta district and the Operator stumbles backwards. Lucy also falls backwards but without the use of her limbs—or any other sign she still has control of her body—she stays standing because of her tenuous connection to the ship. The Operator rushes forward and brings her back to vertical, generating slack in the short cord between her pinky finger and the terminal.

The ship crawls forward until they're past Theta and over WestCorp island, then the end tips down as lightning fills the sky. The roiling bay takes over more of the view through the rain-streaked window. Jirasek, aware of what's happening, struggles against his restraints with a series of grunts. When he realizes he can't break free, he whips his head back and forth with violent nods, his eyes wide.

Their descent gains speed as the forward thrusters go off-line—not free fall, a controlled descent, still traveling forward due to their momentum. The Operator holds on to Jirasek's chair and the back of Lucy's shirt, keeping her in place as best he can. Anything not secured in the ship shifts forward. In the bridge, debris starts sliding forward against the floor, rolling until it hits the bottom of the window or accumulating beneath the console ahead of Jirasek. From somewhere farther in the ship, a dull thud echoes through the hall and into the bridge.

Then, the entire ship goes dark, and Lucy falls limp. Without her limbs spread out, the deadweight becomes more than the Operator can hold—he lets go and she hits the console. The speed of their descent doesn't increase, and they continue their angled trip down to the bay past the island. The Operator lets go of Jirasek's chair and cushions his rapid forward progress with his arms against the console.

"Lucy!" He turns her over and shakes her by her shoulders. Unplugging her from the terminal doesn't change their speed, and he's grateful she kept the thrusters slowing their descent firing.

The Operator throws Lucy over his right shoulder—raising his left arm produces a sharp pain. Then, bent over, he walks back towards the ship's center, each step feeling like he's climbing a mountain trail's steep grade. His arm screams in pain when he grabs the doorframe, but he grits his teeth and ignores it as he pulls himself and Lucy through on their way towards the port.

Each frustrating twist and turn adds more time to the trip and brings the Operator and Lucy closer to impact with the water. He squeezes every drop he can from his broken body, urging it forward faster. His back foot slips whenever he attempts longer strides. His leg muscles are numb but the fresh burns on his shins sting, creating a strange misalignment in sensations.

He gets to the port door as land comes into view in the distance through the port's open side on his right. Turning in that direction, he feels Lucy shift; his right arm isn't strong enough and she tumbles to the ground, his right arm and leg slowing her fall and protecting her head. The ground outside the port looms larger in their view. Mere seconds remain.

The Operator grabs Lucy's right hand with his own, lifts her torso, bends over, and slings her over his back in a fireman's carry. With a roar, he lifts his left arm and wraps one of her legs with it while taking his first steps. He's falling forward on ground angled to the right, each footfall preventing a stumble while he runs to the port's open side.

Impact is at any second. The visible water through the port's open side, first close to land but now halfway to their position, closes in on the ship. The Operator takes the final few steps towards the port's edge and sees streams of water shooting out from beneath the ship where the thrusters force it away. With one final push, the Operator jumps from the falling ship, joining the heavy raindrops that hit the bay's surface.

EPILOGUE

Yoshiko Apocalypse takes a look around Gamma's hazy streets, noting the broken streetlights outside alleys covered in shadow and the layers of graffiti on the crumbling walls. Without her Hololenses feeding her continuous data about the world around her, the sense that she's missing an obvious threat courses through her veins. She quiets the sensation by remembering the rest of the city's inhabitants don't wear the Enforcers' specialized eyewear and they do just fine without them.

But the rest of the city's inhabitants aren't Enforcers.

She approaches the two hovercraft skeletons the old woman in the Gamma market said marked the pool hall's location—an old-style cruiser, and an industrial freighter. There's a brand-new door, matte black metal with a silver sliding peephole and matching silver handles between windows that are yellow with years of neglect and mineral deposits, victims of the persistent haze below the reclaimers.

The sound of yelling men trickles through from beyond the door. For a moment, Yoshiko considers knocking, then remembers that she's still an Enforcer, after all, with or without her Hololenses and exoskeleton. Plus, without aggressive slams of her fist on the door, she doubts anyone would hear her anyways. She turns the heavy silver door handle and walks inside.

Those closest to the door turn and look at the woman standing in the entrance. Not knowing who she is, they stand up straighter, interrupting their ongoing pool game. The pause in action draws the attention of the next row of tables, who look at the new arrival in turn—this continues until every pair of eyes in the pool hall is trained on her except for one: a man with a broom, sweeping with his back to her. Rough men, accustomed to a hard life on the city's ground level, taking a break from life below the reclaimers by enjoying games of pool and glasses of Serum.

"Welcome!" a jovial, heavyset man with a beard says from behind the bar. He hurries around the counter and walks between the rows of pool tables, his eyes darting around at the stationary men. "What are y'all looking at? Never seen a woman before?"

Not one like her, with tattoo sleeves covering both arms. Everyone returns to their games with a grumble.

"Come in, come in," the bartender says. He's wearing a brown button-down shirt, well-worn jeans, and once-white sneakers. He starts ushering Yoshiko through the pool tables before a man lines up for a shot in their path, then takes her around the left side of the room. When they get to the bar, he pulls a barstool out from the counter before scampering around the bar. "Serum?" he says with a smile.

"Sure," Yoshiko responds. Instead of sitting at the offered barstool, she chooses the one on the far left and sits with her back to the wall and one arm resting on the bar. She looks around the room. Everyone's attention is back on their games, and the man with the broom works his way towards the front, pausing when competitors' shots require room in his path.

The bartender sets a full glass of Serum in front of Yoshiko.

"Interested in playing some pool? We've got tables for all levels. New"—he pauses for a moment and raises his eyebrows—"and experienced."

"No games for me, thanks. I'm actually looking for my friends. Heard you might have seen them."

"Your friends? Who are they?"

"Not sure what they're calling themselves these days."

The bartender's smiling face relaxes for a brief moment, a small flicker untrained eyes wouldn't detect.

"A man and a woman. The guy's a little taller than you, athletic, handsome in a rugged sort of way. The woman had short hair last time I saw her, roundish face, high cheekbones, petite. Both good with a blaster. Seen anyone like that?"

The bartender thinks for a moment before grabbing an already clean glass and inspecting it for smudges. He wipes it despite finding none. "Not for a long time," he says, making a point of avoiding her gaze. "I remember two like that though— left Gamma and never came back."

"I see."

A sudden uproar from the table right behind Yoshiko startles her. She whips around, her reflexes taking her hand towards the blaster tucked into her waistband behind her back.

"Did you really think you had a shot?" a man with a red goatee who looks like he sucks lemons for fun says to the crest-fallen man he just beat. He sets his cue stick on the table. "Miguel! I'm ready!" he says, looking at the bartender.

Miguel laughs and sets the double-cleaned glass back with the rest. "You really think so?" he says.

"You said I beat everyone in here again and I get the ace," he shoots back, brimming with confidence.

"Okay, I'll be right back." Miguel sets his rag on the counter and walks through the opening behind the bar. Everyone in the room stops talking for the second time since Yoshiko's been there, punctuated by the rhythmic sound of stiff bristles on the floor. She can hear Miguel from the back. "He said he's ready for you . . . yes, he beat everyone else . . . I don't know, I don't pay attention when he plays."

Miguel reappears and meets the expectant gaze from everyone around the tables. "She said—"

Yoshiko perks up after hearing *she.*

"She'll be right out."

The men all cheer; Miguel smiles.

"Look, I'm sorry I couldn't help you," Miguel says to Yoshiko when he's back behind the bar. There's an undercurrent of expectant chatter throughout the pool hall. "I haven't seen them."

Just then, Lucy appears from the opening in the wall to the side of the bar. Except, she seems different. Instead of wearing the dark gray compression Yoshiko last saw her in, or the crimson jumpsuit from the lost squadron, she has on a black tank top, tight-fitting black jeans, and black boots—the same outfit Yoshiko prefers.

Yoshiko's eyes widen and she closes her mouth when she realizes it hangs open. So the android made it, after all.

"That's—"

"I told you, I haven't seen them," Miguel says with an overpowering, definitive tone in his voice. His eyes bore into her and his jaw flexes, shaking the whiskers on his cheek.

"They don't recognize her?" she whispers, gesturing with her head to the men in the pool hall.

"Recognize who? These men spend all their free time in here—they don't pay attention to what happens in the rest of the city. Or what they broadcast on the billboards."

Yoshiko wonders how many people below the reclaimers never worried about Felipe Jirasek's takeover of the city. From this far down, the problem about *who's* in power doesn't affect them one bit; it's a rigged game that the upper levels convince themselves is fair.

As Yoshiko watches, Lucy walks over to the rack of cue sticks and inspects the options. She reaches a hand out, and her competitor watches with bated breath. Then, she pulls her hand back and turns to the man who earned the right for a game with her.

"Actually, you choose for me," she says. "I don't want you to have a single reason for why you lose."

Lucy looks at Yoshiko, the only other woman in the bar, and winks.

Yoshiko closes her eyes and shakes her head. The challenger chooses an ancient cue stick, held together with bits of tape and glue.

"How'd you know this one's my favorite?" Lucy says.

The challenger shakes his head. "Let's just get to it," he says, pulling the balls from the various pockets while another man puts the triangle on the table.

Yoshiko turns back to the bar and downs her Serum in one long drink, slamming her glass on the table when she's done.

"Can I get you anything else?" Miguel asks Yoshiko.

"No thanks, that's all for me. What do I owe you?"

"It's on the house," Miguel responds. He leans in and lowers his voice. "Enforcers who don't cause problems drink free."

"I'll keep that in mind," Yoshiko says as Miguel pulls away. She stands up from the barstool and starts walking away.

"If I see them, I'll be sure to let them know you stopped by," Miguel says to her back.

Yoshiko lifts a hand without turning around so the bartender knows that she heard him. She turns around near the front door and looks back at Lucy's game.

"Good shooting. Now let me show you how it's done," Lucy says, lining up for her first shot of the game. It's a powerful shot that blasts the blue number two ball into the corner pocket. The cue ball stops with the yellow number one between it and the side pocket.

Yoshiko turns to the door and finds it held open by the man sweeping the floor—the bristles of his broom extend just beyond the bottom of the door.

"Thanks," she says while leaning past the obstruction and looking at the man's face.

The Operator meets Yoshiko's gaze. Then, he holds out his broom and inspects it before looking at the pool hall. "Nothing fancy, but good enough in a pinch," he says.

Yoshiko nods in agreement. She walks out of the pool hall and the door clicks shut behind her.

COULD YOU DO ME A FAVOR?

Please help other readers learn more about this book by leaving a rating and review!

Then head over to my website authormarcoshernandez.com and subscribe to my email list. You'll hear about upcoming releases and deals you don't want to miss!

ALSO BY MARCOS ANTONIO HERNANDEZ

ABOUT THE AUTHOR

Marcos Antonio Hernandez writes from the suburbs of Washington, D.C. An avid reader of both fiction and non-fiction, his favorite authors are Haruki Murakami and Philip K. Dick — in that order.

Marcos graduated from the University of Maryland, College Park with a degree in chemical engineering and a minor in physics. Since graduating, he has worked as a barista, a food scientist, and a CrossFit coach.

authormarcoshernandez.com

www.ingramcontent.com/pod-product-compliance
Lightning Source LLC
Chambersburg PA
CBHW060633260626
47161CB00008B/2877